COSMETIC SCIENCE

For
Final Year B. Pharm. Course
Semester – VIII

As Per New Revised Syllabus

I0647997

Dr. Vrushali S. Kashikar (Kulkarni)
M.Pharm., Ph.D.
Associate Professor & Head,
Dept. of Pharmaceutics,
Modern College of Pharmacy (L),
Moshi, Pune-412105.

Dr. Amol A. Kulkarni
M.Pharm., Ph.D.
Director Research & Professor
CAYMET's Siddhant College of Pharmacy,
Pune-412109.

Dr. Indrajeet D. Gonjari
M.Pharm., Ph.D.
Assistant Professor
(Former Assistant Director,
AICTE, New Delhi)
Government College of Pharmacy,
Ratnagiri.

Dr. Vikram Gharge
M.Pharm., Ph.D.
Principal Scientist
at Emcure Pharmaceutical Ltd.
Pune.

NIRALI PRAKASHAN
ADVANCEMENT OF KNOWLEDGE

N1554

COSMETIC SCIENCE (SEM.-VIII)

ISBN 978-93-86-353-36-8

First Edition : February 2017

© : Authors

Published By :   Polyplate

NIRALI PRAKASHAN

Abhyudaya Pragati, 1312, Shivaji Nagar,
Off J.M. Road, Pune – 411005
Tel - (020) 25512336/37/39, Fax - (020) 25511379
Email : niralipune@pragationline.com

☞ DISTRIBUTION CENTRES

PUNE

Nirali Prakashan : 119, Budhwar Peth, Jogeshwari Mandir Lane, Pune 411002, Maharashtra
Tel : (020) 2445 2044, 66022708, Fax : (020) 2445 1538
Email : bookorder@pragationline.com, niralilocal@pragationline.com

Nirali Prakashan : S. No. 28/27, Dhyari, Near Pari Company, Pune 411041
Tel : (020) 24690204 Fax : (020) 24690316
Email : dhyari@pragationline.com, bookorder@pragationline.com

MUMBAI

Nirali Prakashan : 385, S.V.P. Road, Rasdhara Co-op. Hsg. Society Ltd.,
Girgaum, Mumbai 400004, Maharashtra
Tel : (022) 2385 6339 / 2386 9976, Fax : (022) 2386 9976
Email : niralimumbai@pragationline.com

☞ DISTRIBUTION BRANCHES

JALGAON

Nirali Prakashan : 34, V. V. Golani Market, Navi Peth, Jalgaon 425001,
Maharashtra, Tel : (0257) 222 0395, Mob : 94234 91860

KOLHAPUR

Nirali Prakashan : New Mahadvar Road, Kedar Plaza, 1st Floor Opp. IDBI Bank
Kolhapur 416 012, Maharashtra. Mob : 9850046155

NAGPUR

Pratibha Book Distributors : Above Maratha Mandir, Shop No. 3, First Floor,
Rani Jhanshi Square, Sitabuldi, Nagpur 440012, Maharashtra
Tel : (0712) 254 7129

DELHI

Nirali Prakashan : 4593/21, Basement, Aggarwal Lane 15, Ansari Road, Daryaganj
Near Times of India Building, New Delhi 110002
Mob : 08505972553

BENGALURU

Pragati Book House : House No. 1, Sanjeevappa Lane, Avenue Road Cross,
Opp. Rice Church, Bengaluru – 560002.
Tel : (080) 64513344, 64513355,Mob : 9880582331, 9845021552
Email:bharatsavla@yahoo.com

CHENNAI

Pragati Books : 9/1, Montieth Road, Behind Taas Mahal, Egmore,
Chennai 600008 Tamil Nadu, Tel : (044) 6518 3535,
Mob : 94440 01782 / 98450 21552 / 98805 82331,
Email : bharatsavla@yahoo.com

niralipune@pragationline.com | www.pragationline.com

Also find us on 🅵 www.facebook.com/niralibooks

Dedicated
To
Our
Beloved
Family

Acknowledgement

This book is a positive outcome of **teaching and learning experiences** with the students of Final year B. Pharm course.

My deepest gratitude goes to my **Family**, *Parents, Brother and my daughterand Son* for their full-hearted co-operation, love and moral support. *One can never consent to creep when one feels an impulse to soar.*

I will always be thankful to *The Almighty of GOD* for giving me the strength, will & wisdom tocompile this book.

I wholeheartedly thank and express our profound gratitude towards **Dr. S. N. Dhole** Principal, Modern College of Pharmacy, **Dr. M. D. Burande**, Principal, CAYMET's Siddhant College of Pharmacy, for their valuable guidance.

I am honored to express my profound and deep sense of gratitude towards all my colleagues and Dr. S. B. Gokhale for motivation and support.

I extend my sincere thanks to the all staff of Nirali Prakashan, for completion of this book.

We express our profound and deep sense of gratitude towards Mr. S.B. Gokhale for motivation and support.

We extend our sincere thanks to Mr. Dineshbhai Furia, Mr. Jignesh Furia and all staff members of Nirali Prakashan, for completion of this book.

February 2017

Dr. Vrushali S. Kashikar
Dr. Amol A. Kulkarni
Dr. Indrajeet D. Gonjari

Preface

It is our immense pleasure to present a book of **'Cosmetic Science'**, Semester VIII (Final year) B. Pharm course of Savitribai Phule Pune University, formerly known as University of Pune and all other universities having Cosmetic Science / Technology subject in their curriculum. The insight behind publishing this book is to enlighten the students and to fulfill the needs as per the demand of Cosmetic Science syllabus.

This book covers all the topics of Cosmetic Science, Semester VIII, B. Pharm course. As well said that "The good life is one inspired by love and guided by knowledge", this book is a positive outcome of teaching and learning and industrial experiences of the authors with the students of Final year B. Pharm course since last 10-12 years.

We hope this book will be a valuable reference for researchers, health professionals, cosmetologists and a useful resource for educators and advanced cosmetic science students.

Your co-operation in the form of suggestions are most welcome for the improvement of the contents of this book in due benefits of pharmacy students in further editions.

February 2017

Dr. Vrushali S. Kashikar
Dr. Amol A. Kulkarni
Dr. Indrajeet D. Gonjari

Syllabus

Learning Objectives:

On completion of following theory topics & laboratory experiments, learner should be able to:

- Understand the concepts of cosmetics, anatomy of skin v/s hair, general excipients used in cosmetics.
- Explain formulation of cosmetics for skin, manufacturing, equipments & evaluation of creams like cold cream, vanishing cream etc. & powder cosmetics.
- Explain formulation of cosmetics for hair, manufacturing & evaluation of hair shampoos, tonics etc.
- Describe formulation of cosmetics for eyes, manufacturing & evaluation of eye mascara, shadow etc.
- Understand formulation of manicure products like nail lacquer, remover etc.
- Learn formulation, manufacture & evaluation of baby cosmetics like baby oils, powders etc.
- Explain the concept of cosmeceuticals, history, difference between cosmetics & cosmeceuticals & cosmeceutical agents.

Skills:

- State the correct use of various equipments in Pharmaceutics laboratory relevant to cosmetics.
- Perform formulation, evaluation and labeling of cosmetics like moisturizing cream, vanishing cream etc.
- Perform formulation, evaluation of eye cosmetics, nail lacquer & shampoo.
- Perform formulation, evaluation & labeling of shaving cream, after shave & baby products.
- Describe use of ingredients in formulation and category of formulation.
- Prepare labels as per regulatory requirements.

SECTION-I

1. **Fundamentals and Scope of Cosmetic Science** (08 Hrs.)
   - **Additives in Cosmetics:** Emollients, waxes, oils, humectants, preservatives, binders, surfactants, colours and perfumes.
   - Cosmetics v/s drug formulation. Anatomy and composition of skin and hair. Types of cosmetics.
   - Quality of Water in cosmetic Industry
   - Packaging, Cleanliness, Hygiene and Microbial control in Cosmetic manufacturing
   - Perfumes- Source, classification, blending and fixation

2. **Formulation, Manufacturing & Evaluation of Following Cosmetics** (10 Hrs.)
   - A) **Skin care Products**
     - a) **Cosmetics for skin:** Moisturizing cream, cleansing cream, cold cream, vanishing cream, anti-ageing and anti-wrinkle, antiperspirants, deodorants
     - b) **Powder cosmetics:** Heavy, medium and light powders, compacts
     - c) **Face mask and packs**

d) **Face make up:** Face powder, compact powders, Cake makeup, Liquid makeup, Stick preparation

e) **Coloured makeup preparations:** Lipsticks, Lip balm, Rouge

f) **Suntan & sunscreen preparations.**

B) a) **Shaving preparations:** Formulation of wet shaving, dry shaving and after shave preparations. **(05 Hrs.)**

b) **Bath preparations:** Bath oils, soaps, foams and after bath preparations.

SECTION-II

C) **Hair products:** Shampoos, hair tonics, hair dyes, lighteners, depilatories, shaving preparations. **(04 Hrs.)**

D) **Eye products:** Eye mascara, eye shadow, eye liner, eyebrow pencil **(03 Hrs.)**

E) **Dental care cosmetics:** Dentifrices as powders, paste, gels and Mouth washes **(02 Hrs.)**

F) **Manicure products:** Nail lacquer, Lacquer remover and evaluation tests **(03 Hrs.)**

G) **Baby cosmetics:** Baby powders, oils, lotions, shampoos and soaps **(02 Hrs.)**

H) **Nail care Products:** Nail polish, Nail lacquer, Nail lacquer remover, Nail bleach, nail cream **(03 Hrs.)**

3. **Cosmeceuticals** **(05 Hrs.)**

Introduction, Definition and difference from cosmetics. History of cosmeceuticals. Cosmeceutical Agents - retinoids, hydroxyl acids, beta hydroxyl acids, Antioxidants and others.

Contents

SECTION-II

CHAPTER **1**...

FUNDAMENTALS AND SCOPE OF COSMETIC SCIENCE

1.1 DEFINITION

The term cosmetics have been derived from the term "**COSMETIKOS**" which means the skill to decorate. Thus, cosmetics are the art of decorating yourself to look beautiful. According to D & C Act, cosmetics means any articles meant to be **rubbed, poured, sprinkled or sprayed on** or **introduced into** or otherwise applied to any part of the human body for **cleansing, beautifying, promoting attractiveness or altering appearance** and include any article intended for use as a component of cosmetic. Soap is not covered under cosmetic product.

United States: Defines cosmetics as

- Articles intended to be rubbed, poured, sprinkled, or sprayed on, introduced into, or otherwise applied to the human body or any part thereof for cleansing, beautifying, promoting attractiveness, or altering the appearance and

- Articles intended for use as a component of any such articles; except that such term should not include soap.

European Union: Defines cosmetics as

- "Any substance or preparation intended to be placed in contact with the various external parts of the human body (epidermis, hair system, nails, lips and external genital organs) or with the teeth and the mucous membranes of the oral cavity with a view exclusively or mainly to cleaning them, perfuming them, changing their appearance and/or correcting body odours and/or protecting them or keeping them in good condition".

Definitions are important as they draw a legal line between cosmetics and drugs, determine labeling requirements and other product standards and prescribe the types of claims that manufacturers can make for their products. This distinction is being blurred by a group of products often referred to as 'cosmeceuticals'; however, this term that has no legal definition and is not recognized in any current regulations.

More loosely defined, skin care cosmetics are those that penetrate the top layer of the skin but do not reach the skin dermis and are not absorbed by the blood capillaries. Products that penetrate the dermal layer and are absorbed by the capillary system are classified as pharmaceuticals and are subject to Food and Drug Administration (FDA) safety requirements.

In the strictest sense of the FDA's interpretation, cosmetic products are formulated for the beautification of the skin and should make no claim of performing any drug related functions.

1.2 ADDITIVES IN COSMETICS

1.2.1 Water

It is the main ingredient of cosmetics formulation. Thus, stability and quality of final product is dependent on the purity of water used. Pure water should be used in manufacturing of cosmetics. Pure water on large scale can be manufactured by any of the methods mentioned as follows:

- ✓ Ion exchange system
- ✓ Distillation
- ✓ Reverse osmosis.

1.2.2 Oil, Fats and Waxes

These are used in preparation of creams, lotions, brilliantine, hair oil, lipsticks etc. The source of oil, fat and wax can be mineral source and animal source.

1) Mineral source: mineral oil, paraffin and petroleum jelly

2) Animal source: wool fat, bees wax, Spermaceti.

(a) Oils

Name of oil (Vegetable)	Use in cosmetics
Almond	Creams (emollient)
Arachis	Hair oil, Brilliantine
Castor	Lipstick, hair oil, creams, lotions
Olive	Bath oils, creams, lotions
Light liquid paraffin	Bath oil, hair oil, lotions, creams, brilliantine
Heavy liquid paraffin	Bath oil, hair oil, lotions, creams

(b) Waxes

The commonly used waxes in preparation of cosmetics includes bees wax, spermaceti, ceresin, ozokerite wax etc.

1.2.3 Humectants

This is added to prevent drying out of cosmetics.

Type of Humectants	Examples
Inorganic	Calcium chloride (not used now due to compatibility problems)
Metal organic	Sodium lactate (used in sunscreen lotions)
Organic	Polyethylene glycol, propylene glycol, glycerol, sorbitol, mannitol, glucose

a) **Glycerin:** It is one of the best humectants, producing a shiny, glossy product. It is stable; non-toxic, available from both synthetic and natural sources, and provides a useful sweetening function to the paste.

b) **Sorbitol syrup (approximately 70%):** It is also extensively used throughout the industry and is sometimes considered superior to glycerin depending upon the formulation. It also imparts sweetness and is stable humectants.

c) **Propylene Glycol:** These are more generally used in relatively small amounts in combination with either glycerin or sorbitol. The amount of humectants in any formula obviously has to be adjusted depending upon the other constituents of the formula (especially abrasive nature), but generally the total humectants loading is in the range of 10-30% by weight.

1.2.4 Surfactants

One common feature of surfactant is that they all are amphipathic molecules containing a hydrophobic part and a hydrophilic part, used in cosmetics to impart detergency, wetting, foaming, emulsification and solubilization.

Surfactants on basis of their ionic behavior can be divided into the following four types:

Type of surfactants	Examples
Anionic	Fatty acid soaps, alkyl sulphates, alkyl sulphonates, polyethylene glycol ester, alkyl ether sulphates taurines, sarcosinates etc.
Cationic	Alkyl trimethyl ammonium salts, dialkyl dimethyl ammonium salts, alkyl pyridinium salts, quaternised diamine salts etc.
Non-ionic	Alkanolamides, alkyl polyglycol ether, thioethers, alkyl poly-ethyleneimine amides etc.
Ampholytic	Betains, alkylimidazolines, acyl peptides etc.

1.2.5 Preservatives

Used to prevent spoilage which occurs due to, 1) oxidation of oils and 2) microbial growth.　Unused cosmetics are usually contaminated with *Pseudomonas* but used cosmetics are contaminated with *Staphylococci*, fungi, yeast.

Types of Preservatives:

1) **Antimicrobial agents:** Benzoic acid, formaldehyde, cresol, phenol, thiomersol, phenyl mercuric salts etc.

2) **Antioxidants:** Gallic acid, methyl gallate, BHA, BHT, tocopherol, citric acid, ethanolamine, lecithin, ascorbic acid, sodium sulphite, sodium metabisulphite etc.

3) **Antioxidant synergists:** Enhance the efficacy of antioxidants e.g., ascorbic acid, citric acid, phosphoric acid etc.

4) **UV absorbers:** These are mainly used in products which are vulnerable to visible or UV light. By incorporating UV absorbers colourless containers can be used if deterioration is due to UV light only.

1.2.6 Binders

A binder is added to keep the solid and liquid in the united form and also to maintain consistency.

Type of binder	Examples
1) Dry binder	Zn/Mg stearates
2) Oil binder (water repellant)	Mineral oil, Isopropyl myristate, Lanolin derivatives
3) Water soluble binder	PVP, CMC, Cellulose, Acacia, Tragacanth
5) Emulsion binder	Triethanolamine stearates, Glycerol monostearates

1.2.7 Perfumes

The word perfume has been derived from "per" means through and "fumum" means smoke.

Source of perfume	Examples
Natural (Animal source)	Musk, Civet, Ambergris, Castroreum etc.
Natural (Plant source)	Rose, Jasmine, Lemon, Lavender etc.
Aroma chemical	Eugenol, Farnesal, Rose oxide, Citral, Limonene
Floral base	Rose base, Jasmine base
Woody base	Citrus base (in colognes), spice base, oriental base, fruity base etc.

1.2.8 Colours

Colours can be classified into three classes:

a) **Natural colours:** Plant source: examples, Saffron, Turmeric; Animal source: example, Cochineal (red).

b) **Inorganic colours:** Example, Iron oxides, Chromium oxides, Carbon black, Titanium dioxide, Zinc oxide etc.

c) **Coal tar colours:** Tartrazine, Amaranth, Erythrosine, Indigo carmine etc.

Colouring Agent and Applications

Types of Colouring Agent	Cosmetics Product
Water soluble colour	Bath products (shampoo, shower bath and foam baths), cream, soaps, toothpastes and gels.
Oil soluble colour, pigments	Toothpaste, face make-up, powder, lipsticks and soaps.
Colour lakes	Eye make-up and lipsticks
Water dispersible pigments	Soaps

1.3 COSMETICS V/S DRUG FORMULATION

The legal difference between a cosmetic and a drug is determined by a product's intended use. Under present concept, the boundary at which a cosmetic product becomes drug is not well-defined and different laws and regulations apply to each type of product.

The drugs and cosmetics Act 1940 defines a drug and a cosmetic as;

Drug: "All medicines for internal or external use of human beings or animals and all substances intended to be used for or in the diagnosis, treatment, mitigation or prevention of any disease or disorder in humans or animals".

Cosmetic: "Any article intended to be rubbed, poured, sprinkled or sprayed on or introduced into or applied to any part of the human body for cleansing, beautifying, promoting attractiveness or altering the appearance and includes any article intended for use as a component of cosmetic".

Cosmetic and drug: Some products meet the definitions of both cosmetics and drugs. This may happen when a product has more than one intended uses. For example, a shampoo is a cosmetic because its intended use is to clean the hair. An antidandruff shampoo is a drug because its intended use is to treat dandruff. Among the cosmetic/drug combinations, toothpastes contains fluoride, deodorants that are antiperspirants and moisturizers with sun-protection claims. The claims made about drugs are subject to detailed analysis by the Food and Drug Administration (FDA) review and approval process, but cosmetics are not subject to mandatory FDA review.

1.4 ANATOMY AND THE COMPOSITION OF SKIN AND HAIR

1.4.1 Anatomy and the Composition of Skin

Consumer interest in natural and/or organic cosmetics is growing together with confusing marketing terminology. Natural and organic cosmetics fall into poorly defined and unregulated categories, where an array of different terms are used to present product benefit. Consumers can be easily confused by the nuances of such terms as "natural," "derived from natural materials," "extracts from natural plants," "organic," and "per centage of organic content within the total content of botanical materials." At times, statements are presented in ways that seem to indicate that consumers should seek products that are only 100 per cent natural if they want cosmetic purity or something that is "best." In reality, "natural products" all contain a certain per centage of synthetically manufactured ingredients. In an attempt at differentiation, statements such as "preservative free" are made. However, this is not possible since the addition of preservatives in a cosmetic is a regulatory requirement for product safety and health reasons. "Paraben free" may be the case, but this does not mean the product is preservative free, as the formulation may contain another preservative system that does not have the same long research history of safety as parabens. There have been significant changes in cosmetic formulations since 2000. Dermatological and chemical researchers have increased their understanding of skin physiology, the chemical components of the skin and how these interact with chemicals applied to the skin in the form of cosmetics. The cosmoceutical concept has expanded and become even more sophisticated and effective. Botanically, based products are experiencing a renaissance and renewed credibility as formulations become increasingly sophisticated in their technologies and results. Sunscreens are including more UVA protection and PABA has been practically eliminated from all sunscreen formulations. Animal based ingredients are now replaced with plant based or synthetically manufactured equivalents. Antioxidants are strongly emphasized as a means to prevent skin damage and skin aging. Nanotechnology is coming to the forefront of research and development with unknown limits.

No one can promise a solution to all skin problems, nor can they promise "eternal youth." However, the cosmetic industry is continuously working toward vast improvements in the appearance and health of the skin, while making "aging slowly and gracefully" an attainable and pleasing reality. Cosmetic products and the chemistry behind them can be extraordinarily valuable to the skin. Since, a product's ultimate purpose is to benefit the skin. In order to properly evaluate the positive actions or potential problems of cosmetic products and their ingredients, it is crucial to have an understanding of how the skin works, how and why a product may or may not penetrate it and what care individual skin types and conditions may require.

The skin is a complex, multipurpose organ, one that attracts much attention and scientific study. Science is constantly unraveling the intricacies of skin physiology of the chemical substances present in the skin and of their interaction. This knowledge, in turn, increases the understanding of the process of skin disease and skin aging. Scientists are identifying the skin's individual chemical compounds, the chemical and physiological reactions that accelerate aging. With the aging process better understood, laboratories are developing and incorporating new ingredients into cosmetic products that can reduce or decelerate aging and other skin problems, as well as counteract and/or correct them. A large number of new cosmetic ingredients have been incorporated into cosmetic products in the last 10 years and this is expected to continue at a fast pace. Many of these ingredients are intended to delay the aging process, rejuvenate the skin, improve skin problems and even reduce the risk of skin cancer. An increased understanding of skin physiology allows for more targeted and effective skin care cosmetic formulations.

The Skin's Functions

As the body's largest organ, the skin performs a series of key functions resulting from multiple chemical and physical reactions that take place within it. The skin is a barrier, protecting the body from the elements, injury, and oxidation. It helps to maintain a constant body temperature by helping the body to adapt to different ambient temperatures and atmospheric conditions through the regulation of moisture loss. It gathers sensory information and plays an active role in the immune system, protecting from disease. In order to play all of these functions: protective, metabolic, sensory and immunological, the skin must maintain its own auto-repairing capacities and functional integrity. Cosmetic products are very important to the skin's protective function. Sunscreens protect against UV radiation and, therefore, against premature skin aging and skin cancer. Creams and lotions with a bactericidal effect reduce and/or control excessive proliferation of bacteria on the skin, a problem particularly associated with oily skin and one of the main causes of acne development. By forming an invisible barrier on the skin's surface, specific moisturizing ingredients can help to reduce the skin's moisture loss that results in dehydration. The skin also protects internal organs from exposure to oxygen. Without the skin, the body's organs would rapidly oxidize; much like a peeled banana or apple does when its interior is left exposed to air. Through the secretion of sweat and sebum, the skin performs an excretory function, eliminating a number of harmful substances resulting from the metabolic activities of the intestine and the liver. The skin also secretes hormones and enzymes. When the skin's chemistry and chemical composition are not compatible with a particular product's ingredient(s), the result is overall product sensitivity and even allergic reactions. The large number of nerve endings in the skin makes it sensitive to touch. As a result, the skin is a sensory organ and the of receptivity for cold, heat and pain. The skin plays an immunological role, primarily through the Langerhan's cells, which carry antigens from the skin to the lymphatic system. Excessive UV radiation either destroys or inhibits the performance of Langerhan's cells, increasing the risk of skin cancer.

The Skin's Components and Structure

The skin has a very intricate micro anatomical structure. In addition to thousands of skin cells, within one square inch of skin, varying from 0.04 inches (1 mm) to 0.16 inches (4 mm) in thickness, there are some 650 sweat glands, 65 hair follicles, 19 yards of capillaries, 78 yards of nerves, thousands of nerve endings, Merkel cells for sensory perception and Langerhans cells for immunological protection. The skin also contains melanocyte cells responsible for producing the melanin that gives the skin its colour and pigmentation spots, or freckles. The skin is home to a variety of glands. These glands are important not only because of their intrinsic functions but also because they represent a route of entry into the skin for certain chemical compounds. Their main function is to synthesize substances that can cool the body, protect the skin, increase skin suppleness, or eliminate impurities such as mineral elements or cholesterol. Among these glands are the sebaceous glands and two sweat glands: the eccrine and apocrine glands. Sebaceous glands, also known as oil glands, are attached to the same duct that contains the hair follicle. They are responsible for oil secretion in the skin and are held within little sacs. The ducts of the oil glands open into the upper portion of the hair follicle. Usually, there is only one oil gland per follicle, but in some locations there may be more, resulting in greater oil (sebum) secretion in that area. Oil glands are found in almost all parts of the body. The face and back contain the highest number per square inch of skin, whereas the palms of the hands and soles of the feet contain none. The sebum secreted by the oil glands lubricates the skin and helps to prevent the evaporation of moisture. It also possesses antifungal properties. Excessive oil secretion is associated with the development of acne, while insufficient oil secretion is associated with skin dryness. Sweat glands are abundant throughout the skin. Eccrine glands are the most numerous. Their secreting duct opens as a pore directly onto the skin surface. Very abundant on the soles of the feet and the palms of the hands, they secrete a transparent fluid composed mainly of water, lactic acid, urea, toxins and even bacteria fighting substances.

The primary function of this secretion is to cool the body and to maintain thermal equilibrium with the environment. The apocrine sweat glands are situated in the axillae, the eyelids, the pubic area and the genitals. They are inactive until puberty and are stimulated by the emotions and stress. The apocrine sweat gland's excretion is very limited; it does not occur directly onto the skin's surface, but rather into the upper part of the phylosebaceous orifice and from there to the skin surface. The perspiration from apocrine sweat glands can smell unpleasant due to a chemical reaction between the excretion, oxygen and the enzymes produced by the microflora of the hair follicle. It is important to note that dirt, impurities and the asphyxiation or clogs, seen in the pores occur in the hair follicle. They are the result of a mixture produced by oil and the keratinized and corneocyte cells present in the follicle. Cleansing the skin means eliminating impurities from these pores.

Perspiration is not a cleanser. It may help to clean the tiny opening of the sweat pores, but perspiration will not cleanse the hair follicle pore, the pore through which oil is secreted. This is a regular misconception by those who feel that saunas or perspiration cleanse the skin. The surface of the skin is acidic. Its pH, also known as its protective mantle, is formed by a number of components. On the stratum corneum, these include naturally secreted sebum and perspiration (which contains lactic acid), as well as chemical reactions that occur in the epidermis, generating several relatively strong water soluble acids. At the stratum corneum, the skin's pH level ranges from 4.4 to 5.6, depending on the individual and the place on the body from which the reading is taken. It also appears to vary by individual and race. As one moves past the stratum corneum through the epidermis and into the dermis, the pH level increases and becomes neutral (pH 7.0) at the dermis. This process is not completely understood.

The skin's acidity helps to maintain the strength and cohesiveness of the skin, helps ward off infection by preventing the growth of bacteria and allows for easier and more normal exfoliation of surface dead cells. One of the principal reasons why soaps, especially harsh soaps or cleansers with high pH values are detrimental to the skin is because the skin needs an acidic environment to function properly. Thus, after the use of certain skin care cleansers, the use of a balancing lotion is needed. When cleansers have a neutral or alkaline pH, the skin's acidic level needs to be restored. Left alone, the skin will regain its acidic value in about 20 minutes or more depending on the level of acidic imbalance created. Sensations, such as cold, heat, pressure, vibration and stretching (both of skin and tendons), result from a stream of nerve impulses detected and transmitted to the brain by encapsulated nerve endings. All of these components and actions are found within the basic building block of skin tissue, treated and discussed as three layers.

The Skin's Layers

The skin is a highly specialized and complex set of tissues divided into three layers: the epidermis, the dermis and the hypodermis, also known as the subcutaneous layer. There are several different types of cells in the skin, the most important of which are keratinocytes, melanocytes, fibroblasts, immune competent cells (Langerhan's cells), migrating mononuclear cells and mastocytes. In addition to these various cell types, the skin also contains connective tissues that are rich in Extra Cellular Matrix (ECM), the components of which are primarily responsible for the flexibility of the skin its suppleness and elasticity. Other physiologically important functions such as hydration, temperature regulation and the regulation of the skin's permeability depend on specific cells and the chemical composition of the ECM. These regulatory functions are closely linked to the interaction between the cells and the chemicals in the skin through special receptors located on the cell's membrane. The epidermis is the part of the skin visible to the naked eye. It is a very thin layer: its thickness varies from 0.63 inches (1.6 mm) on the soles of the feet to 0.002 inches (0.04 mm) on the eyelids. The epidermis contains a variety of cells, including keratinocytes which are engaged in a constant process of reproduction to replace exfoliated cells; Langerhan's cells for immunological protection; melanocytes for skin colour; and Merck cells that are involved in the function of touch. This is the layer of skin to which products are applied and the one with which an individual (and cosmetics) comes most in contact when cleansing, exfoliating, healing, or hydrating.

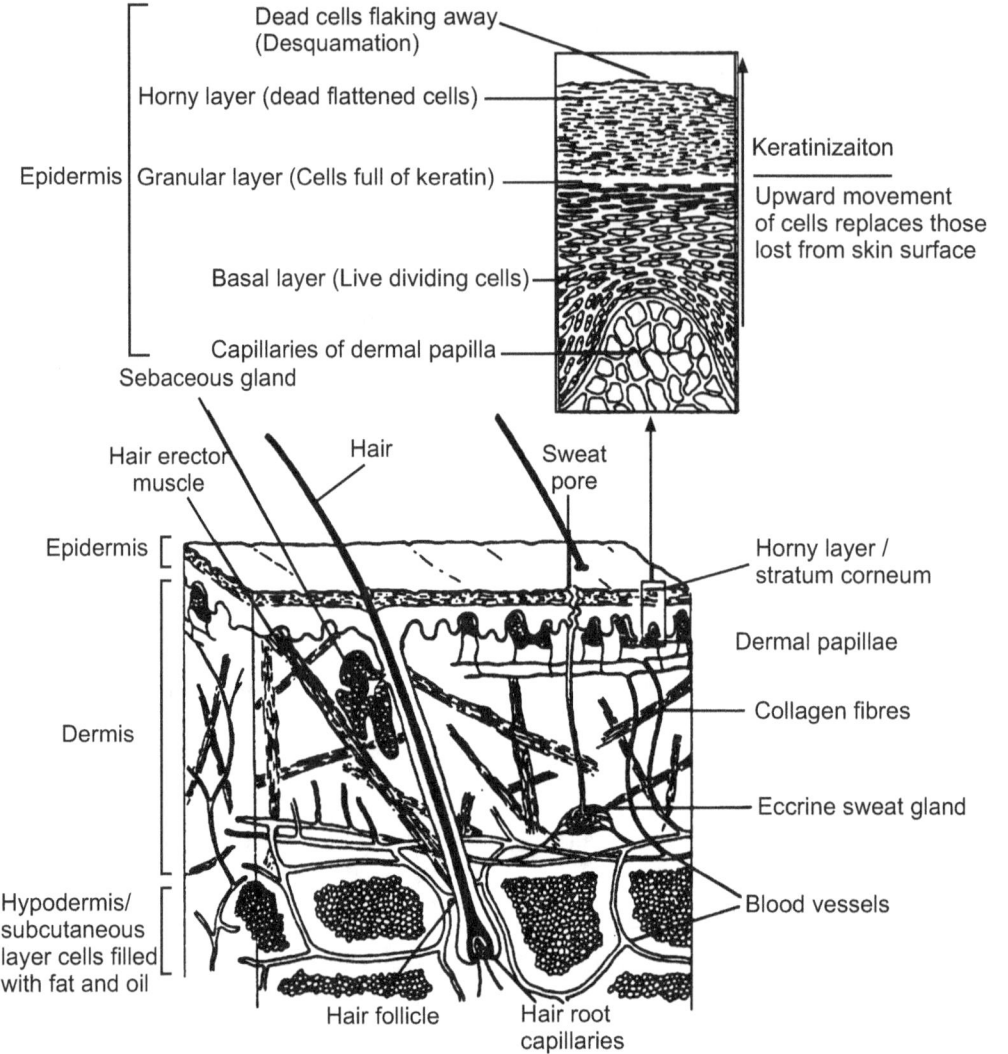

* Note : Sensory nerve endings have not been included

Fig. 1.1

The second skin layer, or dermis, lies below the epidermis and is connected to it by the basement membrane. The dermis represents the most important part of the skin. It is made of connective tissues, collagen, elastin, hair follicles, sebaceous glands, sweat (eccrine) glands, blood vessels and nerves that transmit sensations of pain, itch and temperature. There are also specialized nerve cells that transmit the sensations of touch and pressure. The third skin layer, the hypodermis, is the deepest of the three layers. Consisting primarily of connective and fatty tissues, the hypodermis is much thicker than the dermis. Its measured thickness, however, depends on the part of the body being evaluated and the fat content of the individual. This layer is important for body temperature regulation. A close examination of each layer, including composition and function, is important for further understanding of the impact a cosmetic product may have on the skin.

1) The Epidermis

The epidermis gives the skin its glow, youthfulness, texture and good looks. It is responsible for the health of the skin, protecting it from moisture loss and the penetration of bacteria. Ultraviolet rays, an acne condition, visible skin disease, cigarette smoke, pollution and skin cancer all affect this layer. It is a metabolically active tissue that synthesizes the lipids and contains all the individual components required to form the protective barrier layer. Since, the epidermis represents the outermost layer of the skin, it acts as the initial barrier to oxidant assault. The epidermis has a higher protective and antioxidant capacity than the dermis because it stores essential free radical scavengers such as vitamins E and C and superoxide dismutase. This layer also contains large amounts of glycosaminoglycans and ceramides. The epidermis is further divided into five sublayers of cells, all metabolically very active. From the surface of the skin down to the dermis, these five layers are:

1. Corneum layer
2. Lucidum layer
3. Granulosum layer
4. Spinosum layer
5. Germinative layer

The epidermal cells are formed in the germinative layer and move upward toward the corneum layer. In their upward process, epidermal cells undergo a number of chemical modifications, transforming from soft, protoplasmic cells into flat surface "scales" that constantly rub off.

The epidermis holds a large amount of water. The layer with the highest water content is the germinative layer, holding about 80 per cent. Each subsequent layer has less water as a per centage of its total chemical composition, with the corneum layer containing only 10 to 15 per cent water. Water is held in the cell's cytoplasmic gel and in the intercellular channels (spaces between the cells). The younger the body, the more water there is in the skin. The skin's capacity to retain water decreases with age, making the skin more vulnerable to dehydration and wrinkles.

The epidermis is also the first barrier against immunological aggressors, thanks to the Langerhan's cells. These dendritic cells are formed in the bone marrow and migrate to the skin's dermal and epidermal layers. Once they complete their migration, Langerhans cells typically are found in the lower layers of the epidermis, comprising about 5 per cent of the total epidermal cell population. These cells engulf foreign bodies, carrying the invaders to the lymphatic system to be processed and eliminated. Langerhans cells are sensitive to ultraviolet radiation and are easily damaged by UV rays. Even minor UV exposure will damage the Langerhans cells enough to reduce the skin's immune capacities. With age, these cells also decrease in number. This is one reason why the potential rate of skin disease increases with age. In a young person, it takes approximately 28 days for a cell to travel from the germinative to the corneum layer. With age, the speed of this process is greatly reduced. It is estimated that after the age of 50, it takes about 37 days to complete the same process. Put in terms of skin aging, this indicates that stimulating skin functions, either manually through facial massage or through cosmetic product activity, would improve cellular metabolism. The 28 and 37 days time span is also important when it comes to skin sensitivity and the misuse of facial scrubs. If it takes 28 days or more for a cell to reach the surface of the skin, then we are naturally exfoliating one layer of dead cells a day. Depending on the harshness of the material, the use of scrubs may remove more layers of surface dead cells than appropriate, potentially increasing skin sensitivity. Furthermore, the misuse of scrubs may exacerbate oil gland activity, thereby increasing oil production, the opposite of what the user generally wishes to achieve.

Epidermal Layers

The primary function of the epidermis is to manufacture the uppermost layer, the corneum layer. An improperly functioning keratinocyte formation system cannot generate a cosmetically acceptable corneum layer. Therefore, an important factor for beautiful skin appears to be the appropriate metabolism of keratinocytes in order to generate a healthy corneum layer. This is important in order to protect against moisture loss and the penetration of bacteria and microbes. The germinative layer, also referred to as the basal layer, is where the cells reproduce by mitosis: one cell divides into two, creating two cells identical to one another and to the original parent cell. After subdivision, one cell remains in the basal layer and the other is pushed upward toward the mucosum layer.

In young skin, the germinative layer is the thickest layer of the epidermis. Here, the cells are large and supple and contain a high per centage of water. As the cells move upward, they begin to fill with a granular substance called keratin. The keratinocytes lose water, become flatter and their nucleus begins to degenerate. They secrete "cement" made up of lipids, cholesterol, free saturated fatty acids and ceramides into the intercellular spaces, increasing cohesion between the cells and thereby contributing in making the epidermis an effective barrier. In their last state of migration, the cells reach the corneum layer. In healthy, young skin, it is made of 18 to 23 layers of flattened, dry cells (corneocytes) firmly cemented together. The actual number of layers depends on a variety of factors, including oil secretion and the skin's own desquamation system. The stratum corneum is thicker on the palms of the hands and soles of the feet. The corneum layer includes a Natural Moisturizing Factor (NMF) made of hydrosoluable (able to dissolve in water) and hygroscopic (able to retain water) substances that regulate the corneum's selective permeability. A well-formed stratum corneum tends to be thin and compact, with an orderly cellular structure, or basket-weave and strong barrier function. This is normal in young, healthy skin. When the corneum layer is thick and its cells are arranged in a scaled, uneven pattern, the natural barrier action of the skin is reduced, allowing for faster substance penetration. This is one reason why products may have a burning sensation on skin that is very dry and scaly. When the skin is excessively moist, sensitivity also may occur because the "barrier" has been softened, resulting in increased ease of product penetration. For aging or damaged skin, ingredients such as alpha hydroxyacids (AHAs) tend to restructure an abnormal stratum corneum, giving it a healthier and normal basket-weave structure. Skin pigment or melanin is formed at the deepest layer of the epidermis by the melanocyte cells. This pigment is later transferred to the keratinocytes, giving the skin its colour. Excessive melanin production is induced either by UV light exposure (e.g., sun bathing, tanning beds) or hormonal imbalances.

Immunological protection is provided in the epidermis by the Langerhans cells. Their function is to detect foreign bodies that have penetrated the epidermis, capture them and carry them to lymphocytes in the lymphatic system. An immune response is then triggered, neutralizing and finally eliminating the foreign element. Touch is sensed by the Merkel cells that are situated between the keratinocytes. These three specialized epidermal cells, the melanocytes, the Langerhans cells and the Merkel cells, account for 13 to 20 per cent of total epidermal cells.

2) The Dermis

The dermis is the second layer of the skin. It is 10 to 40 times thicker than the epidermis. Within the dermis are the appendages of the skin, the hair follicles, sebaceous, two sweat glands (eccrine and apocrine glands), plus a complex capillary and nerve network. It is made of 80 per cent moisture, elastin tissues that supply elastic properties and collagen fibres that provide a structural framework. Collagen represents about 70 per cent of the dermal proteins and provides resistance, resilience and traction. About 20 different types of collagen fibres have been identified. In addition to collagen and elastin, the dermis has a variety of other fibres, grouped together as structural glycoproteins and a set of chemicals grouped under the term glycosaminoglycans. These are responsible for hydration, suppleness and water retention. They also regulate permeability, provide resistance to pressure and are responsible for the orientation of proteins. By means of its vast network of capillaries and blood vessels, the dermis provides energy and nutrition to the epidermis and plays a critical role in healing and thermoregulation. It is responsible for the supporting framework and elasticity of the skin, which also depends on a well-balanced water content in the dermis and other skin layers. To facilitate this essential hydration, the dermis acts as a water storage site. It also protects the body from mechanical injury and plays an important role in sensory perception and as an internal regulator. Langerhans cells, responsible for immunoprotection, are also present in the dermis. Collagen and elastin protein fibres, the two main components of the dermis, act as a structural support system for the nerve fibres, hair follicles, blood vessels and oil and sweat glands located in this layer and also provide the skin with strength and elasticity.

The proper functioning of the dermal layer, as well as its water content, accounts for the skin's smoothness and elasticity. A properly functioning dermis is key for a youthful appearance and beautiful skin.

3) The Hypodermis

The hypodermis, the skin's third and last layer, connects the skin with the muscle tissues. This layer is highly elastic and has fat cells acting as "shock absorbers," thereby supporting delicate structures such as blood vessels and nerve endings. The hypodermis may be regarded as the extension of the strong fibrous and elastic bundles forming the dermis. For the skin to be healthy and beautiful, balance and the proper working of all interrelated elements is essential.

1.4.2 Anatomy and the Composition of Hair

Macroscopic and Microscopic Structures of the Hair

Hair is a derivative of the epidermis. Externally, hair is thin, flexible tubes of dead, fully keratinized epithelial cells, whereas inside the skin, it is a part of individual living hair follicles, cylindrical epithelial down growths into the dermis and subcutaneous fat, which enlarge at the base into the hair bulb surrounding the mesenchymal derived dermal papilla. From a macrostructural point of view, hair varies in length, diameter, colour and cross-sectional shape among the different ethnic groups and among singular individuals. Hair has two separate structures: the follicle in the skin and the hair shaft, which is visible on the body surface. The hair shaft consists of a cortex and cuticle cells and in some cases, a medulla in the central region. The medulla is the central part of the hair, whereas the cortex, which represents the majority of the hair fibre composition and plays an important role in the physical and mechanical properties of hair, is the peripheral part and is made up of approximately 50–60% of macrofibrils, which consist of rods of microfibrils embedded into a matrix. The hair shaft cuticle covers the hair from the root to the tip of the epidermis and is formed by flat overlapping cells. Each cuticle cell is generally 0.3–0.5 µm thick and its visible length is about 50 µm; it consists of various sublamellar structures (the epicuticle, A-layer, exocuticle, endocuticle, and inner layer) and the cell membrane complex. The integrity and properties of the cuticle layer have an important role in protecting the cortex from physical and chemical insults and in maintaining the hair in a clean and disentangled state and have a great impact on its appearance.

1.5 TYPES OF COSMETICS

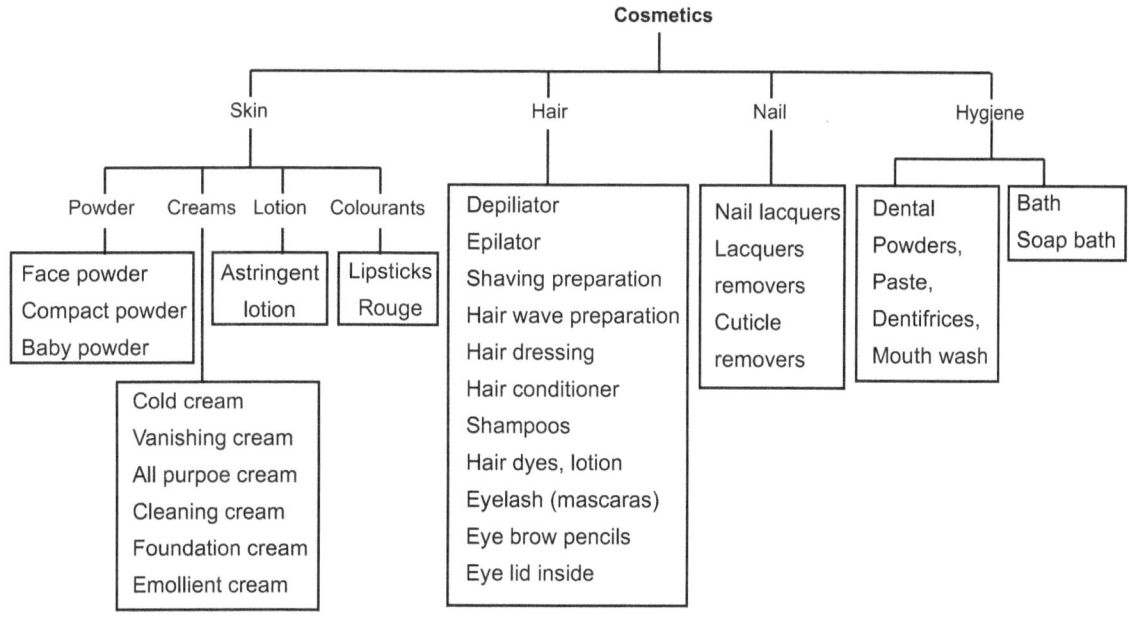

1.6 QUALITY OF WATER IN COSMETIC INDUSTRY

Water is one of the major commodities used by the cosmetics industry. It finds usage in the cosmetics industry at various stages. It may come directly in contact with the finished products, as excipients or vehicle or it may exist as an integral part of the formulation. It may either be initially used in the preparation of a product but may later be removed or may only be used as cleansing agent for rising vessels equipment, primary packaging etc.

Different grades of water are required depending on the requirement of different formulation stages. Control of the quality of water, in particular microbiological quality, is a major concern and the cosmetics industry must pay considerable importance to the development and maintenance of water purification systems.

Though water is a cheap ingredient as compared to other ingredient used in cosmetics formulation, it is important that whenever water is used in cosmetics, its quality is controlled, as it may be the biggest source of contamination in the products. The quality of water to be used in cosmetics should be not less than purified water used in the pharmaceutical industry.

Purified water is obtained from potable water, which is feed water to the purification system. It goes through various stages of purification to give purified water. The primary treatment includes filtration, passing through activated carbon beds and addition of chemical additives/water softeners. Deionization, electro deionization and electrodialysis then improve chemical quality attributes of water by removing cations and anions. Reverse osmosis, ultrafiltration and distillation gives higher quality of purified water.

The various techniques that can be used to prepare purified water are

- Ion exchange
- Reverse osmosis
- Distillation
- UV radiation

To produce water of controlled and repeatable clarification according to fixed standard, some combination of filtration, softening, deionization or distillation is necessary. The capabilities of each process vary according to the input water quality and equipment design of an efficient treatment process. Feed water quality varies in the following aspects:

- Hardness of water
- Level of organic compound
- Chlorine content
- Conductivity
- Bioburden

The grades of water used at different stages in the manufacture of cosmetic products should be discussed in the manufacturing dossier. Validation and qualification of water purification, storage, and distribution system are a fundamental part of GMP and form an integral part of the GMP inspection.

1.7 PACKAGING

The packaging of skin care products serves for product protection but also is intended to persuade people to buy. The four main aspects that matter for the selection of a cosmetics container are the type of container, compatibility, functionality and the protection of the products. The packaging of skin care products serves for product protection but also is intended to persuade people to buy.

Primary packaging materials for cosmetics have to be carefully developed or must be selected from amongst materials already on the market. A basic requirement of packaging is the protection of the contents of the pack. In particular there must be an adequate barrier against water vapour, UV light, oxygen and CO_2. Furthermore, it must be assured that no components or ingredients of the packaging can migrate into the product, and there must be no adsorption or absorption of components from the product into the packaging. In addition the packaging must be non-hazardous, i.e. it must not contain any toxic substances, as well as not being capable of transmitting any substance into the product which may be in a potentially toxic concentration. Furthermore, the packaging material must be suitable for routine processing; the required output and a constant quality level have to be ensured.

Legal Requirements for Cosmetics Packaging

It may be necessary to add some effective type of device to prevent fraudulent or counterfeit copying, as well as childproof packaging, especially where it is required for medicinal products and in the case of natural cosmetics, ecological credentials and sustainability of the packaging can be highly relevant. Further aspects to consider are functionality, convenience and other demands related to the specific market.

Besides the basic purpose and the microbiological and physical aspects, also the compatibility of container materials and content is of significance. Stability measurements are carried out over a longer period though before the container material is actually used.

1.8 MICROBIOLOGICAL CONTROL OF FINAL PRODUCT

Microbiological durability depends on product composition, content of preservatives, manufacturing hygiene, packaging, transport and storage. The ability of microorganisms to grow and reproduce in cosmetic products is well known. Water is essential for microbial growth and water based products often have a limited durability, as they are sensitive to microbial growth. More cosmetics are ideal nutrient media for microorganisms.

Microbial Contamination during Manufacturing

Contamination during production and filling in cosmetic products may occur. Raw materials can contribute to a significant level of microbial contamination to the finished product. Testing of raw materials before use, especially those of natural origin is important. The specifications of the raw materials must include microbiological purity. Water is a raw material and the most common ingredient. Water must be tested continuously for microbial growth. It might be necessary to sterilize deionised water to obtain a sufficient purity. Many other conditions of production may influence the contamination during manufacturing, such as contaminated areas, insufficient manufacturing hygiene, personnel hygiene and insufficient preservation.

Microbial Contamination after Opening

From the moment of opening the cosmetic product is subject to constant and variable microbial contamination from the domestic environment and the consumer's hands and body (the skin). Since, microorganisms are ever present in the home, especially in warm, moist areas, such as bathrooms and kitchens, cosmetics are exposed to contamination with both spoilage and potentially hazardous microorganisms during use.

Preservation

The purpose of preservation is for consumer protection and prevention of spoilage during normal and reasonable product use. The preservatives inhibit the growth of contaminating microorganisms during manufacturing, storage and use by consumers after opening. Preservatives must be used at the lowest concentration that ensures their efficacy and this must be determined during the product development process. The efficacy of antimicrobial preservation in cosmetics can be tested with the challenge test. The use of preservatives in cosmetics cannot replace good manufacturing practice.

Preservative Challenge Test

Antimicrobial challenge test that determines the antimicrobial effectiveness of a preservative in a formulation or an unpreserved product formulation against selected test microorganisms.

Method

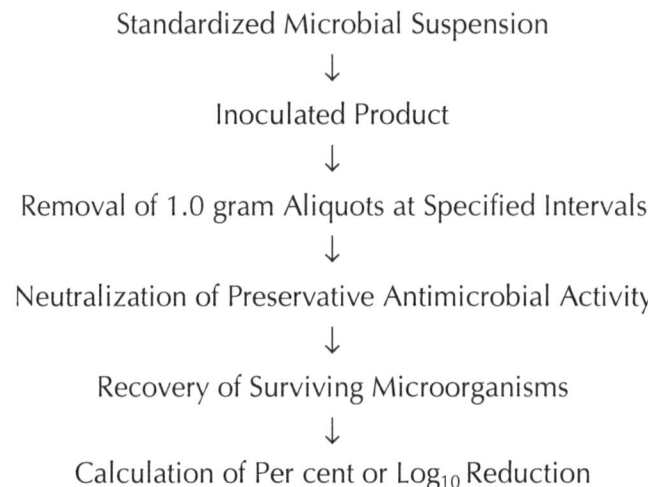

Standardized Microbial Suspension
↓
Inoculated Product
↓
Removal of 1.0 gram Aliquots at Specified Intervals
↓
Neutralization of Preservative Antimicrobial Activity
↓
Recovery of Surviving Microorganisms
↓
Calculation of Per cent or Log_{10} Reduction

Formulation Factors: Water and Microbial Growth

Water is necessary for microbial growth to occur. Microorganisms will only proliferate in the water phase of a product formulation.

- In emulsions, microorganisms will grow in the aqueous phase, but will also collect at the interface between the oil and water phases of the formulation.
- To prevent microorganisms from growing, a traditional or a non-traditional/alternative preservative has to be present in the aqueous phase of a product formulation. Two ways for incorporating a limited water soluble preservative into an aqueous product formulation,
- Use a water miscible solvent to dissolve a water insoluble or limited water soluble preservative.
- Use heat to warm up the water phase of a product formulation to dissolve a water insoluble preservative. Parabens are more soluble in water at 80°C than at 25°C.

Oil and water soluble preservatives will migrate or naturally partition themselves between the water and oil phases of a formulation.

By migrating into the oil phase of a formulation, there might not be a sufficient concentration of the preservative in the water phase where microorganisms are located to protect the formulation.

In such cases remedies are limit the solubility of the preservative by adding 10% or more of glycerin, ethanol, butylene glycol, hexylene or by adding greater than 5% of propylene glycol to the water phase of the formulation.

1.9 HEALTH HAZARDS IN COSMETIC PRODUCTS

Safety Issues Pertaining to Cosmetics

The Indian consumer has the "right to be protected against marketing of goods and services which are hazardous to life and property" (Consumer Protection Act 1986).

Since, the dawn of civilization cosmetics have constituted a part of routine body care not only by the upper strata of society but also by middle and low class people. Since, few decades there is a big boost in cosmetic industries, by the production of the various types of the cosmetics which are needed for the care and beautification.

In recent times attention has been focused on cosmetics, disinfectants and other personal body care products as major sources of heavy metals in human systems. Metals in nail polishes reach the body through the porous keratinized nails. Research in metal concentration of cosmetics is raising awareness on direct ingestion and skin absorption of metals, since they are daily used and are applied to the thinnest areas of facial skin, such as the pre-ocular areas and lips, where absorption is very high.

Heavy Metals in Cosmetics

Heavy metals are naturally occurring, are present in the environment and can make their way in trace quantities into raw materials. These substances end up in the products we consume and use every day. They can be found in pigments and other raw materials in all industries including the cosmetics industry. Some include the preservative thimerosal (mercury), the progressive hair dye lead acetate and a number of tattoo pigments such as red cinnabar (mercuric sulfide). Metals have been found as contaminants in a range of cosmetic products including sunscreen, foundation, nail polish, lipstick and whitening toothpaste. Heavy metals like lead, arsenic, mercury, aluminium, zinc, chromium and iron are found in a wide variety of personal care products including lipstick, whitening toothpaste, eyeliner and nail colour. Some metals are intentionally added as ingredients, while others are contaminants. Exposure to metals has been linked to health concerns including reproductive, immune and nervous system toxicity. While some metals are contaminants of the chemical combining process, others serve as colourants. For instance, chromium is used in a very small number of products as a colourant, and iron oxides are common colourants in eye shadows, blushes and concealers. Some aluminium compounds are colourants in lip glosses, lipsticks and nail polishes. In addition, some colour additives may be contaminated by heavy metals, such as D&C Red 6, which can be contaminated by arsenic, lead and mercury.

Dermal exposure is expected to be the most significant route for cosmetic products since the majority of cosmetics are applied to the skin. Dermal absorption of heavy metals is typically low, with absorption of individual elements influenced by a number of factors including physical-chemical properties of the mixtures. Oral exposure can occur for cosmetics used in and around the mouth, as well as from hand to mouth contact after exposure to cosmetics containing heavy metal impurities. Inhalation exposure is expected to be negligible.

Assessment of dermal absorption by a single component in a cosmetic product is complex and depends on factors such as the concentration in the product, the amount of product applied, the length of time left on the skin and the presence of emollients and/or penetration enhancers in the cosmetic product. Given this complexity, and the lack of well-conducted dermal absorption studies incorporating these factors, determination of heavy metal limits in cosmetics based on human health risk alone is a challenge.

Some of cosmetic preparation having the heavy metals are : Kajal, Lipstick, Nailpolish, hair which are explain below:

Kajal

Fig. 1.2

Eyes are one of the most delicate and sensitive organs of the body and protecting them from harmful external factors. Various ingredients go in the making of cosmetics. While most of them may be fine for our skin, there are still some ingredients that can cause possible damage to the eyes. Most commercially produced kajal contain high levels of lead. Studies have revealed that kajal comprises of galena (PbS), minium (Pb_3O_4), amorphous carbon, magnetite (Fe_3O_4), and zinc oxide (ZnO). Prolonged application may cause excessive lead storage in the body, affecting the brain and bone marrow, causing convulsions and anemia. While the rules of mentioning the ingredients in a product on the label are rather strict in the US, in India, they are a little relaxed. Cosmetics are regulated under the Drugs and Cosmetics Act 1940 and Rules 1945 which state that there is no need to mention the ingredients label on cosmetic packs of less than 60 ml for liquids and 30 g for solids and semisolids. This poses a problem for eye cosmetics as they generally come in smaller packs. What one needs to be careful about while buying eye make-up is to avoid products which contain mercury, lead and parabens. These are extremely harmful and their prolonged usage can cause various health hazards and may even lead to blindness in some cases. You may not be able to notice any problems initially but using it regularly will lead to deposits of harmful chemicals in your body. In order to avoid this, opt for branded products where you can check with the store or company about the ingredients in the product and discard it if it irritates your eye or skin at any point.

Lipstick

Fig. 1.3

The primary ingredients found in lipstick are wax, oil, alcohol, and dye. Though, lead is not an ingredient of the lipsticks, it might be present as impurities in the colour additives. The type of pigment used in lipsticks also contributes to its heavy metal content. No lipstick lists lead as an ingredient. The amounts are small, but the presence of lead in lipstick, which is ingested and absorbed through the skin, raises concerns about the safety of a cosmetic product that is widely popular among women. Urged on by both consumers and the cosmetics industry, the U.S. Food and Drug Administration conducted its own testing in 2010. The FDA results were even more astonishing: The agency detected lead in all 400 lipsticks tested, ranging from 0.9 to 3.06 ppm four times higher than the levels observed in the study done by Campaign for Safe Cosmetics. The FDA said, "We have assessed the potential for harm to consumers from use of lipstick containing lead at the levels found in both rounds of testing. Lipstick, as a product intended for topical use with limited absorption, is ingested only in very small quantities. We do not consider the lead levels we found in the lipsticks to be a safety concern." Likewise, the cosmetics industry also does not see this as an issue, saying that the dose makes the poison, in other words, the trace amounts of heavy metals in lipsticks are not harmful. But the FDA noted, "Although we do not believe that the lead content found in our recent lipstick analyses poses a safety concern, we are evaluating whether there may be a need to recommend an upper limit for lead in lipstick in order to further protect the health and welfare of consumers". Indeed, what the FDA and the cosmetics industry have been ignoring is cumulative exposure and potential long-term adverse effects.

It is true that a single lipstick application will not lead to harm. And the good news is that not all lipsticks contain detectable levels of lead or other heavy metals. The problem is when women who wear lipstick apply it two to 14 times a day. Women are not only applying lipsticks several times a day, but they also are doing this in the span of a whole lifetime, which means that exposure to lead and other heavy metals adds up and can potentially affect their health.

Nail Polish

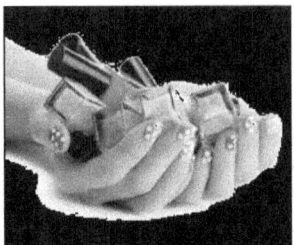

Fig. 1.4

Small amounts of metals are present in most of the polishes and may cause exposure if nails are bitten or chewed and the polish ingested. The formulation starts with a synthetic polymer solubilized in a chemical solvent. Various additives can be used to alter the flexibility / hardness of the film and other characteristics of the polish. Dyes and pigments are solubilized or suspended into the solution to provide a wide variety of colour options and effects. Chemicals which are most concerning are the solvents (solubilizers) and plasticizers. Two specific ingredients whose safety has been called into question are the Plasticizer, Dibutyl phthalate and solvent, Toluene. The colourants typically used are either synthetics or iron oxides which may contain heavy metals.

Hair Colour

Fig. 1.5

While hair dyes have always been a witches brew of chemicals, two specific compounds may be responsible for the increased risk of non-Hodgskins lymphoma and other cancers. Phenylene diamine is not the only hazard found in hair dyes. Coal tar colours, which are listed on hair dye labels as FD&C or D&C colours, are derived from the tar found in bituminous coal. The problem is that this thick tar also contains a number of toxic contaminants, including benzene. Some coal tar colours also contain heavy metals impurities, including lead and arsenic, both of which cause cancer and can disrupt hormones. Although many of the synthetic colours used in hair dyes have never been tested for safety, the World Health Organization considers them all possible carcinogens.

CHAPTER 2...

SKIN CARE PRODUCTS

2.1 INTRODUCTION

The word cream signifies a solid or semi-solid emulsion. If an emulsion is of much low viscosity that, it can be poured under influence of gravity alone, it is termed as lotion. (An emulsion is dispersion of one immiscible liquid in the other). Water is an important ingredient of skin creams and lotions as moisture content of the skin controls the appearance of skin. Therefore, in skin creams or lotions, either fatty phase (oil) can be dispersed in aqueous phase (water) or aqueous phase can be dispersed in fatty phase. If oil droplets are dispersed in aqueous phase (water) emulsion is termed as oil-in-water (o/w) and if water is dispersed in fatty phase (oil) emulsion is termed as water-in-oil (w/o). It has been observed that o/w emulsions occasionally change into w/o emulsions and vice-versa.

To make dispersion of one phase into the other, suitable emulsifying agents are used. Most of them belongs to the class of surface active agent, these substances possesses both hydrophilic (affinity for water) and lipophilic (affinity for lipids) properties. It is because of this property that these can be held at an oil-water interface, lipophilic portion oriented towards the oil and hydrophilic portion oriented towards the water.

A large number of surfactants are available. It is often difficult to select a most suitable emulsifies. William C. Griffin devised the HLB (Hydrophilic Lipophilic Balance) System. This system is used to indicate the behavior of an emulsifying agent depending upon the proportion of hydrophilic and lipophilic groups present in the molecule of the emulsifying agent.

An emulsifying agent with low HLB value tends to be lipophilic in character and forms water in oil emulsions and an emulsifying agent with high HLB value tends to be hydrophilic in character and forms oil in water emulsions. HLB values, however, give indication only of the behavior characteristics of the material and do not indicate emulsion stability.

A combination of lipophilic and hydrophilc surfactant, often, is found more useful than a single surfactant. HLB values of combinations can be calculated by taking weighted averages of the individual HLB value of surfactants. A combination of sorbitan monostearates (HLB 4.7) and polyoxyethylene sorbital mono-oleate (HLB 15) in ratio 68 : 32 will exhibit an average HLB value of 8 ($0.68 \times 4.7 + 0.32 \times 15 = 8$).

Water sensitive polymers are useful as auxiliary emulsifying and thickening agents. Natural or synthetic clays are commonly used for building viscosity of emulsion or for suspending solids such as pigments e.g. bentonites, attapulgite etc. Some naturally occurring gums and synthetic hydrophilic polymers (e.g. gum arabica, gum-tragacanth and polyoxyethylene polymers, carboxyvinyl polymers) are useful as emulsifiers as well as emulsion stabilizers.

There is direct relationship between emulsion viscosity and the viscosity of continuous phase. Three interacting effects must be balanced by an emulsion formulator to control emulsion viscosity. These are

1. The viscosity of both o/w and w/o emulsions can be increased by reducing the particle size of dispersed phase.

2. Reduction in particle size results in improvement of emulsion stability.

3. Flocculation or clumping which tends to structure the internal phase can have stabilizing effect.

As a general use, the viscosity of emulsions increases upon ageing. Cosmetic emulsions contain a number of ingredients such as carbohydrates, proteins, sterols etc. which support growth of microorganisms. Contamination may be introduced by the consumer during its use therefore it is necessary to include preservative in cosmetic emulsions.

Preservative should possess the following properties:

(1) Low toxicity

(2) Stability to storage

(3) Chemical compatibility

(4) Acceptable odour and colour

(5) Reasonable costs

(6) It should be effective against a variety of microorganisms.

Concentration of preservatives will depend on its extent at which it is available to interact with microorganisms. Microorganisms can reside in both phases i.e. aqueous phase and fatty phase. Therefore, preservatives should be available in effective concentration in both the phases. It is almost impossible for a single preservative to distribute itself in effective concentration in both the phases. Problems may arise when one of the ingredients interact with preservative thereby rendering the preservative ineffective. Cosmetic creams are usually marketed on the basis of their broad claims, made on their packaging.

Most commonly available creams classified on the basis of their function are :

(a) Cleansing cream

(b) Cold cream

(c) Massage creams

(d) Night creams

(e) Moisturizing creams

(f) Foundation creams

(g) Vanishing creams

(h) Hand and body protection creams

(i) All purpose creams

2.2 MOISTURIZING CREAMS AND LOTIONS

When water is lost from stratum corneum more rapidly than it is received from lower layers of the skin, the skin becomes dehydrated, the dehydrated skin loses its flexibility and appears rough. Water (moisture) plasticizes stratum corneum, provides flexibility and makes it soft. Soft skin appears smooth. Those creams which restore water (moisture) to the stratum corneum are called moisturizing creams. Water contained in the cream is lost by evaporation when the cream is applied to the body. Therefore, a moisturizing cream must provide a non-volatile residual film capable of retaining the moisture of the skin as well as moisture which is applied directly by the cream. Emollients imports smoothness and general sense of well-being to the skin, as determined by touch e.g. glycerin, sorbital, propylene glycol, ethoxylated derivatives of lipids, hydrocarbon oils, waxes, silicon oils, vegetable oils, fats etc.

Ingredients	Per cent of Total
Stearic acid	4
Mineral oil	8
Lanolin	1
Glyceryl monostearate	3
Isopropyl myristate	2
Glycerin	4
Propylene glycol	4
Triethanolamine	0.2
Water to make	100
Perfumes and preservatives	q.s.

Ingredients	Per cent of Total
Cetyl Alcohol	2
Mineral oil	8
Glyceryl monostearate	7.5

Isopropyl myristate	1
PEG 400 monostearate	10
SLS	0.2
Glycerin	5
Propylene glycol	3.5
Triethanolamine	0.2
Water to make	100
Perfumes and preservatives	q.s.

Evaluation

1. Colour
2. Odour
3. Texture
4. Spread ability
5. Consistency
6. Appearance

2.3 CLEANSING CREAMS AND LOTIONS

Functions of cleansing cream/lotion are removal of facial make-up, surface grime oil, dead cells and crusts. Although water is good and cheap cleansing agent but it is ineffective on its own against oils. Soap can emulsify oils and therefore, soap and water can effectively remove oil, but disadvantages of this combination are,

- It is inconvenient outside the bath room.
- It may remove too much oil from skin surface leaving it rough and dry.
- Residual alkalinity of soap may cause outermost cells to lift and separate from neighboring cells.

These disadvantages can be overcome by properly formulated cleansing cream or lotion. A cleansing cream should have the following properties:

- It should be stable and should have a good appearance.
- It should spread easily without dragging.
- During application it should not have oily or greasy feel.
- After evaporation of water the cream residue should not become viscous.
- Its physical action should be that of flushing on the skin and pore opening rather than absorption.
- A thin emollient film should remain on the skin after its use.

Though bees wax-borax emulsions are develops very easily and now a number of other materials are available for formulation of cream but these emulsions still occupy an important place in cleansing creams.

Mixture of natural wax and vegetable oil is used, but because of unsaturation present in vegetable oil it is unstable. So it is replaced by mineral oil. Inclusion of borax into formulation enhances stability of emulsion.

Bees wax has two disadvantages:

(a) It has distinctive smell, its odour is not unpleasant but it is not compatible so it has to be masked into the final product.

(b) As it is obtained from natural sources, it differs in its quality and cost depending on their source of origin and time.

When a borax solution is mixed with molten bees wax, sodium salts of the wax acids will be formed at the oil water interface. It is usual to use rather less than the theoretical quality of borax since this gives a more stable, textured creams. Usually, 5-6% of the weight of bees wax is used.

Ingredients	Per cent of Total
Bees wax	10
Mineral oil	40
Ozokerite wax	10
Paraffin	12
Borax	0.5
Water to make	100
Perfumes and preservatives	q.s.

Ingredients	Per cent of Total
Bees wax	8
Mineral oil	50
Microcrystalline wax	5
Borax	0.4
Water to make	100
Perfumes and preservatives	q.s.

Certain non-ionic surfactants are commonly used which enhances flexibility and stability of emulsion e.g. sorbitan sesquioleate, sorbitan stearate.

Ingredients	Per cent of Total
Bees wax	10
Mineral oil	48
Lanolin	4
Borax	0.7
Sorbitan sesquioleate	1
Water to make	100
Perfumes and Preservatives	q.s.

Ingredients	Per cent of Total
Bees wax	8
Mineral oil	20
Lanolin	3
Borax	0.5
Hydrogenated vegetable oil	27
Sorbitan stearate	5
Polysorbate 60	2
Anti-oxidant	0.5
Water to make	100
Perfume and Preservative	q.s.

A number of bees wax derivatives are manufactured with modified emulsifier properties. Ethoxylated bees wax derivative available with HLB values ranging from 5 to 9. Although they still have the bees wax odour, it is claimed that creams made from them are softer, liquefy readily, allow the incorporation of larger amounts of water, are neutral and stable at 50°C.

Skin has a protective sebum layer which is buffer on acid side. Skin returns to normal pH quicker if acid cleansing creams are used. However, there is limitation of emulsifying agents which will make stable acid cleansing creams. Emulsifying agents that can be used in formulation of acid cleansing cream are glyceryl stearate, cetyl or stearyl alcohols, phosphated fatty alcohols. Citric acid, lactic acid, lemon juices are some of the acidic substances that may be used in acid cleansing creams.

Ingredients	Per cent of Total
Wool wax	4
Lonolin	7
Stearyl alcohol	2
Petrolatum	35
Glycerin	5
Lactic acid	1.5
Water to make	100

Bees wax-Borax type cleansing creams are difficult to remove with water alone. In contrast with such cream washable cleansing creams can be prepared with detergents as part of emulsifying system.

Ingredients	Per cent of Total
Mineral oil	38
Ozokerite	2
Cetyl alcohol	2
Sodium cetyl sulphate	1
Water to make	100
Perfumes and preservatives	q.s.

A cream having gel like texture can be prepared from formula. This gel will cleanse well and can be rinsed off the face with water.

Ingredients	Per cent of Total
Stearic acid	10
Mineral oil	25
Triethanolamine lanolate	5
Terpineol	0.05
Lanolin (anhydrous)	3
Propylene glycol	6
Water to make	100
Perfumes and preservatives	q.s.

Cleansing Lotions

Cleansing lotions have been more popular after the introduction of polyethylene plastic containers. Lotions spread in thin layers and because of this sometimes are more economical. Lotions have stability problems.

There are two basic types of cleansing lotions. The simplest type of lotion is a solution or emulsion of a detergent in water. For example a 5% solution of triethanolamine laury sulphate in water or 10% emulsion of sulphonated olive oil in water.

To stabilize the formulation besides emulsifying agent, auxiliary emulsifying agents like glyceryl monosterate, fatty alcohols, bees wax etc. are used.

Ingredients	Per cent of Total
Mineral oil	38
Bees wax	2
Triethanolamine stearate	8
Water to make	100
Perfumes and preservatives	q.s.

Another problem with lotions is viscosity. Viscosity during preparation can be adjusted with water if more viscous lotion has resulted. If the resultant product has low viscosity, viscosity can be improved with materials like triethanolamine stearate. Since triethanolamine stearate discolour on standing, it is advisable to make triethanol amine stearate *in situ* by using calculated amounts of triethanolamine and stearic acid. For one part of triethanolamine two parts of stearic acid is used.

Oil in water type of cleansing lotions have tendency to increase in viscosity with ageing. Ethoxylated cholesterol can be used to retard this problem.

Ingredients	Per cent of Total
Stearic acid	3.5
Cholesterol	0.5
Ethoxylated cholesterol	0.3
Glyceryl monostearate	2
Mineral oil (light)	27
Triethanolamine	1.5
Propylene glycol	5
Water to make	100 ml
Perfume and preservatives	q.s.

If the product is meant for oily skin with active substances like salicylic acid, and resorcinol, sulphur may be added. Another approach for preparing cleansing products for oily skin is to use solvents like ethyl or isopropyl alcohol in concentrations upto 60%. Pre-saturated pads of these solvents are also available. Concentration of alcohols should not be more than 60% or else it will cause excessive drying and irritation. Harsh effect of alcohol should be modified with emollient.

Ingredients	Per cent of Total
Alcohol (ethyl alcohol)	12
Menthol	0.05
Camphor	0.1
Cetyl dimethyl benzyl ammonium chloride	0.2
Ethoxylated cetyl alcohol	2
Stearylamine	1
Water to make	100
Perfumes and preservatives	q.s.

2.4 COLD CREAM

In cosmetic industry, cold creams consist of creams in solid water-in-oil emulsion form that is made by using bees wax and alkali, usually borax as emulsifying agent.

The emulsifying agent used in the cold cream is in-situ soap formed by the interaction of borax with the free acid of the bee wax. Borax or sodium tetraborate is usually marketed as a decahydrate $Na_2 B_4O_7$. $10H_2O$ Cold cream must primarily have an emollient action. Also it should produce a cooling sensation and the resultant oil film on the skin should be non-occlusive.

Traditionally, cleansing creams are of two types:

(a) White, emulsified cold cream

(Bees wax-borax type)

(b) Translucent, anhydrous in character.

Bees wax – Borax type

Basically, this is oil-in-water type of emulsion. After the creams are rubbed on the skin, a sufficient quantity of water evaporates to impart a phase inversion to the water-in-oil type. The solvent action of oil imparts cleansing properly.

General Procedure for Manufacturing:

The ingredients are divided into, a) Oil phase, b) Aqueous phase.

a) **Oil phase:** The ingredients of oil phase should be taken in increasing melting point. Add the oil or wax gradually in increasing melting point and melt with continuous stirring.

b) **Aqueous phase:** Take separately the ingredients of aqueous phase and mix them and heat to same temperature. Mix the aqueous phase with the oil phase with continuous stirring.

Ingredients	Per cent of Total
White bees wax	7
Paraffin wax	10
Ceresin wax	3
Mineral oil	44
Borax	1
Water to make	100
Perfume	0.5

Evaluation

- Consistency (Rheology/viscosity)
- Spread ability
- Homogenity
- Texture
- pH

2.5 VANISHING CREAMS

Creams which spread easily and seem to disappear rapidly when rubbed on the skin are termed as vanishing creams. These creams are composed of emollient esters which leave little apparent film on the skin. Low per centage of oil phase is also chosen for the above mentioned reason. Traditional formulae of vanishing creams are based on stearic acid. Stearic acid melts above body temperature and crystallizes in a form so as to be invisible providing a non-greasy film. Stearic acid also imparts attractive appearance to the cream. With stearic acid, white creams are produced and sometimes because of this whiteness these creams are called 'snow'.

Ingredients	Per cent of Total
Stearic acid	17
Potassium hydroxide	0.7
Glycerin	5
Water to make	100
Perfumes and preservatives	q.s.

Creams prepared with such formulae contain partly saponified stearic acid, free stearic acid and water. These creams leave a dry, tacky, residual film. This film also has a drying effect on skin. Such creams are suitable for hot climates which causes perspiration on the face.

The texture of cream also depends on amount of stearic acid saponified and alkali used. Cream made with NaOH is harder than those made with KOH. Borax is another alkali that can be use to make cream. Creams produced with borax are very white in colour but the product has tendency to become grainy. Triethanolamine is an excellent alkali. Balancing this and fatty acid variation can be made and other emollients can be added easily. Glycerin where used in soap creams should not exceed 10%. Since, these soap creams contain a large amount of water these are liable to lose water by evaporation and therefore, should be packed in airtight containers.

Self emulsifying glyceryl monostearate can also be used as emulsifying agent in preparation of vanishing creams. The advantage of using self emulsifying glyceryl monostearate is that it is not having drying effect on skin as is the case with creams prepared with alkali stearates.

Ingredients	Per cent of Total
Mineral oil	2
Cetyl alcohol	3
Glyceryl monostearate	15
Glycerin	10
Water to make	100
Perfumes and preservatives	q.s.

For dry and flaky skin some special oily materials like lanolin, lanolin derivatives are used in vanishing creams.

Ingredients	Per cent of Total
Glyceryl monostearate	12
Mineral oil	4
Cetyl alcohol	2
Lanolin	1
Glycerin	6
Water to make	100
Perfumes and preservatives	q.s.

2.6 ANTI-WRINKLE OR ANTI-AGING CREAMS

Anti-wrinkle or Anti-aging creams are predominantly moisturizer based cosmeceutical skin care product marked with the promise of making the consumer look younger by reducing the visible wrinkles.

Formulation I

Anti-wrinkle preparations of 1960s are based on bovine serum albumin and form an invisible mask over the skin. They are allowed to remain in contact with facial skin for about 6–8 hours i.e. for the period of time during which they remain effective.

Manufacturing

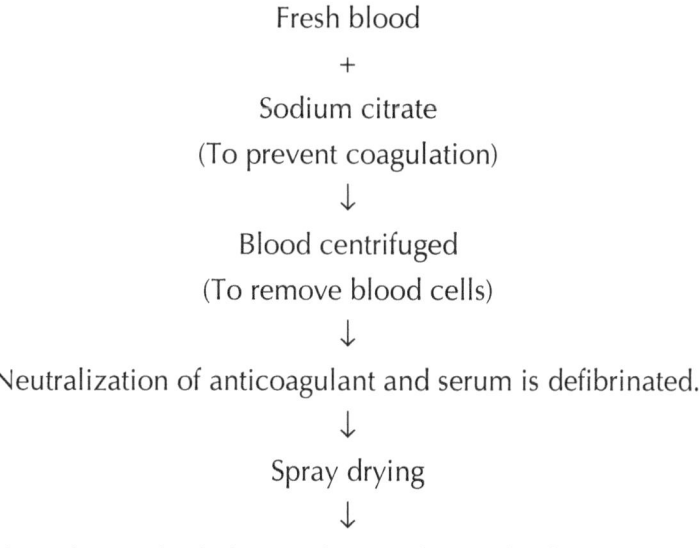

Fresh blood

+

Sodium citrate

(To prevent coagulation)

↓

Blood centrifuged

(To remove blood cells)

↓

Neutralization of anticoagulant and serum is defibrinated.

↓

Spray drying

↓

Product obtained is light in colour and completely water soluble

The smoothing effect which follows the application of the preparations would seem to be purely physical, one entailing the filling-in of facials wrinkles and the formation of tight occlusive film which stretches the skin. The effect is largely depending on how much the facial muscles are used.

Formulation II

A wrinkle smoothing composition by an American patent contains proteins obtained from cow's milk, namely α-lacto albumin and some β-lacto globulin. The film produced with this composition is claimed to be effective for about 4 hours and can be re-activated by moistening it with little water. Both the proteins are unsaturated and water soluble.

(i)   Protein (4 : 1) in H_2O -   10–30%

(ii) Water   -   70–90%

(iii) Plasticizer (Non-toxic) -   2–4%

(Example: Glycerin or propylene glycol to increase flexibility of dried films)

pH of final product is in between 5 to 7.

Recent Formulation of Anti-aging Cream is Olay total effects anti-aging cream.

2.7 ANTIPERSPIRANTS

Perspiration is a phenomenon in which regulation of body temperature and protection of skin from dryness occurs. Perspiration takes place because of sweat gland.

There are two types of sweat gland:

(i) **Eccrine Gland:** Occur over almost all body surfaces and open on skin surface through a thin duct.

(ii) **Apocrine Gland:** These are associated which sexual development and occur after puberty.

The secretion by eccrine gland is highly dilute aqueous solution. The secretion of apocrine gland is oily sticky materials. Sweat from both eccrine and apocrine glands are odourless when discharged, later, sweat from apocrine gland which contain fatty substances like lower fatty acids, steroids, lactones etc. are decomposed by resident bacteria producing odorous substance.

Way to Control / Reduce Odour

➢ Reduction in apocrine sweating.

➢ Removal of secretions of both types of sweat glands as quickly as possible

➢ Control bacterial growth

➢ Absorption of body odour

Commonly used Aluminium and Zirconium salts are

• Aluminium Chlorhydrate

• Aluminium chloride

- Aluminium Sulphate
- Zirconium chlorhydrate

Since, the odour is produced by the bacterial action on sweat, so antibacterials which are used are:

- Benzethonium chloride
- Chlorhexidine acetate
- Hexane acetate
- Triclosan
- Ethyl alcohol can be used as a solvent

Formulation

Several materials with astringent preparation has been used as antiperspirants. Aluminium chlorhydrate has pH of 4.0–4.5 which is close to pH value of skin surface. As it can damage the fabric, fabric damage inhibitor like urea/borax can be included in formulation. Aluminium chlorhydrate solutions are made by adding small amounts of powder to water and mixing well. It is available as 50% aqueous solution. It is miscible which ethanol, propylene glycol and glycerin.

Antiperspirants can be formulated in the form of liquid cream, lotion, thick and powder.

a) Liquid Antiperspirants

These are aqueous or hydro-alcoholic solution of astringent salt with humectants. Alcohol present tends to prevent hydrolysis of astringent in solution. They are applied by sprays and rollon. Quaternary ammonium salts e.g. cetyl pyridinium chloride, cetyl triethyl ammonium bromide i.e. cetrimide or chlorhexidine are used as a deodorant in antiperspirants.

Ingredients	Per cent of Total
Part A	
Alcohol	50
Propylene glycol	5
Hexachlorophene	0.1
Perfume	q.s.
Part B	
Aluminium chlorhydrate	15
Water to make	100

b) Cream Antiperspirant

They are vanishing cream type. It should contain at least 15-20% of astringent salt. Acid stabilized glyceryl monostearates can be used as emulsifier, other non-ionic emulsifier are spans and tweens. Other fatty materials like cetyl alcohol, white petroleum jelly and mineral oil can be added in small amounts. Fabric damage inhibitor is used. For example, urea 5-10%. Humectants like glycerin, propylene glycol, sorbitol in concentration of 3-10% is used. Titanium dioxide is used as opacifier/whitner. Perfume use should be acid stable. Glycine is used as a buffer for fabric protection. Glycine is more stable than urea under normal storage conditions.

Ingredients	Per cent of Total
Isopropyl myristate	32
Bentone (Modified bentonite)	7
Ethyl alcohol	3
Zirconyl Hydroxy chloride	5.5
Silicone	1
Perfumes	q.s.

c) Lotion Antiperspirants

They are very similar to cream. Lotion should be tested for stability. It contains GMS, mineral oil, petroleum jelly, spermaceti wax, aluminium chlorhydrate etc.

Ingredients	Per cent of Total
GMS	15
Mineral oil	5
Petroleum jelly	2.5
Spermaceti wax	5
Glycerin	6
Aluminium chlorhydrate	40
Water to make	100
Perfumes	q.s.

d) Stick Antiperspirant

They contain wax like matrix which acts as carrier for aluminium chlorhydrate and volatile silicone.

Ingredients	Per cent of Total
Volatile silicone oil	45
Aluminium chlorhydrate	20
Stearyl alcohol	24
Polyethyleneglycol Distearate (6000)	6
Polyethylene glycol 1000	2

e) Powder Antiperspirant

They can be prepared by mixing antiperspirant salt with talcum powder.

Ingredients	Per cent of Total
Aluminium sulphate buffer	8
Aluminium lactate	8
Talcum powder to make	100
Perfumes	q.s.

Manufacturing of Antiperspirants

Antiperspirant lotion and cream are manufactured according to general method. Incorporation of astringent salts in cream and lotion should be controlled to avoid breaking of emulsion. Emulsion stability should also be tested on aging.

Waxy antiperspirant sticks can be manufactured by blending antiperspirant salt and other solid materials in a base and pouring the molten mixture into the mould.

Liquid antiperspirants are marketed as aerosols which contain propellant with suitable container and valve. Alcohol is used as solvent. Selected perfume should be tested for compatibility at room temperature and slightly elevated temperature (40-45°C). The finish products are tested for skin irritation or sensitization test.

In powders, all ingredients should be mixed and grinded to get uniform dispersion. The active ingredients should be dissolved in solvent and distributed throughout the powder mixture. Perfume blended with talcum powder can be added.

Compatibility of deodorant and perfume should be studied. Many non-ionics (emulsifiers) inhibit the activity at antibacterial. Therefore, compatibility of emulsifier and antibacterial agent should be carried out.

Evaluation

Antiperspirant product should be capable of sweat reduction by 20%. Efficacy of an antiperspirant is defined as Per centage reduction in the rate of sweating in the axilla that may be achieved after a realistic application or a series of application of the test product.

I) Gravimetric Method

- Test involves use of shaved axillae not exposed at any antiperspirant before one week.
- Tared absorbent pads are placed on dry axillae.
- The pads are retains for half an hour.
- This procedure is repeated for 3-6 times to obtain specific data.
- The number of repetition and collection of data depends on reproducibility of the ratios of weight of perspiration from the right axilla to left. This is known as PR i.e. perspiration ratio.
- In the afternoon of the same day the product is applied to axilla which perspired the most. After one hour, preweighed pads are applied to both the axillae, 3-6 collections can be made. PR is calculated. This is repeated for next 3 days.
- The effectiveness can be calculated by comparing the data relation between each day with control data.
- Another back-test method is more rapid and convenient.

II) Hygrometry

- Electronic hygrometer enables to get accurate results. In this method, a cup is attached to the skin and the water from the enclosed area is evaporated by a stream of dry gas.
- The water content of this gas stream is monitored and the sweat rate is calculated.
- Since, the cell used to cover the skin is not very large and only enclosed a small area in the axilla, the positioning of this probe is very critical.

2.8 DEODORANTS

A wide variety of products which are deodorants and not antiperspirants have been successfully marketed. The various forms in which deodorants are available are,

- Sticks
- Powders
- Soaps
- Sprays

Ingredients	Per cent Range
Hexamethyl enetetramine	14-20
Zinc oxide	16-23
Starch	16-23
Petroleum jelly	38-43
Perfume	0.5-1.2

i) Deodorants Soaps

The deodorant soaps are classified as drugs and (USA) as antimicrobial agents are used in soaps. The most frequently used antimicrobial agents in soaps are trichlorocarbanilide (TCC), triflurocarbon (CF_3) and triclosan.

ii) Deodorants Powders

In deodorant powder, it is essential that the active ingredient should be uniformly distributed. This can be done by mixing and grinding. If active ingredient is liquid then it can be sprayed over adsorbent powder.

Ingredients	Per cent of Total
Talc	67
Precipitated chalk	12
Boric acid	5
Zinc oxide	5
Zinc phenol sulphonate	1
Perfume	q.s

iii) Deodorant Creams

A potassium stearate, stearic acid, vanishing cream, serves as a base for making deodorant creams.

Ingredients	Per cent of Total
Part A	
Isopropyl Myristate	2
Cetyl Alcohol	2
Stearic Acid	4
Glyceryl Monostearate	10
Hexachlorophene	0.3
Part B	
Potassium hydroxide	1
Propylene glycol	12
Water to make	100
Perfume	q.s

Method

- Heat all ingredients of part A at 75°C till melted.
- In another container, heat all the ingredients of part B at 75°C with quick agitation.
- Add perfume when temperature of preparation is 40°C.

iv) Stick Deodorants

Deodorants are also appeared in the form of stick. They can be formulated as alcohol based gels or on alcoholic ingredient. Generally, hexachlorophene or bithonol is used as an ingredient. The formula consists of 5-10% of sodium stearates alone or with other hard soap, 2-5% of humectants, alcohol and perfumes. The gel is formed by dissolving soap in warm alcohol. Stirring should be rapid enough to dissolve the soap.

Ingredients	Per cent of Total
Sodium stearate	08
Propylene glycol	10
Coconut diethanolamide	68.8
Tricloson	0.2
Water to make	07
Colour and perfume	q.s

Ingredients	Per cent of Total
Part A	
Stearic acid	06
Ethyl alcohol	64.75
Part B	
NaOH	01
Water	05
Part C	
Hexachlorophene	0.25
Propylene glycol	02
Ethyl alcohol	18
Perfume	03

Method

- Mix all the ingredients of part A and heat till 70°C.
- Dissolve NaOH in water (part B) and heat till 70°C.

- Mix all the ingredients of part C till dissolved and heat till 70°C.
- Transfer and mix hot solution of part B to part A at 70°C with rapid agitations.
- A clear soap solution should be end result.
- Add the solution of part C to this mixture and mix well and pour into moulds.

Evaluation of Deodorants

The nature of axillary odour is due to bacterial degradation of apocrine secretion. Apocrine glands are larger and more numerous in the axilla. Gram positive bacteria are associated with typical axillary odour. Micro cocci produce sweaty acidic odour. Deodorants are evaluated by both *in-vitro* and *in-vivo*.

The two principal methods for the *in-vivo* evaluation are,

1) Determination of the effect of treatment on the skin micro flora and

2) Olfactory assessment of the effect on skin odour.

The different techniques which are used to quantify micro flora are,

- Tape stripping
- Contact plates
- Velvet replicate pads
- Swabbing
- Scrubbing
- Pressurized spray method

Odour Evaluation

- Test involves, on first day record odour of both axillae.
- The product under test can be applied to one of the axillae and one is treated as control.
- After 6 hours both axillae again check and odour are recorded.
- A particular odour is used as a benchmark and odour of the test are compared for evaluation of deodorant preparation.

Skin Sensitization

The substances that induce inflammation are called irritant substances. Irritants are of two types.

1) **Primary irritants:** Cause inflammation on first contact and may be for several hours.

2) **Secondary irritants:** They are harmless on first contact but cause inflammation on repeated contact and become more severe with progressive contact.

Tape Stripping Method

In this methods, scotch tape is applied on the surface and stripped. This is then dipped in a nutrient media, incubated and growth of any colonies of bacteria is monitored.

2.9 POWDERS COSMETICS

Powders cosmetics are categorized as face powder, body powder and compacts.

The powders should have the following properties:

- Must have good covering power so can hide skin blemishes.
- Should adhere perfectly to the skin and not blow off easily.
- Must have absorbent property.
- Must have sufficient slip to enable the powder to spread on the skin by the puff.
- The finish given to the skin must be preferably of a matt or peach like character.

The raw materials used to manufacture of various powders are classified with examples as follows,

Raw Material for Powder Imparting	Examples
Covering properties	Titanium dioxide, ZnO, Kaolin, Zn stearates
Adhesion properties	Mg Stearates, Talc, Mg and Ca salt of Myristic acid
Slip and Softness	Aluminium hydrosilicate
Absorbency properties	Starch, Colloidal Kaolin, Bentonite, Precipitated chalk
Peach like finish	Rice starch, Silica, Powdered silk
Frosted look	Guanine, Bismuth Oxychloride, Mica, Zn, Al
Colour and perfumes	Iron oxides

Ideal Characteristics of Powders

1) **Covering power and Playtime:** Covering power is calculated from the refractive indices. Materials of high refractive index and relatively small particle size are referred in the preparation of face powders. Playtime is the amount of time that the makeup can be moved on the face prior to sitting.

2) **Slip:** It is the quality of easy spreading and application of powder.

3) **Adhesiveness:** How well the powder will cling to the face?

4) **Absorbency:** Eliminate shiny skin in certain facial areas by absorbing sebaceous secretion and perspiration.

5) **Bloom:** Ability to impart a velvety peach like finish to the skin.

Face Powder: Types of face powders are,

A. Loose face powder

B. Compact face powder

C. Talcum / Body powder

D. Baby powder

2.9.1 Loose Face Powder

The essential features of a good face powder includes, covering power, slip, adhesiveness, absorbency, bloom, Colouring, perfuming.

Types of Face Powder	Purpose and Composition
Light	Dry skin, contains large amount of talc
Medium	Normal or moderately oily skins, lesser talc and Zinc oxide
Heavy	Extremely oily skins, low talc but higher amount of Zinc oxide

Excipients

I. Adhesives and Covering Agents

1. Talc

- Particles should pass through a 200 mesh screen.
- Easy slip and low covering.

2. Kaolin (China clay)

- Good covering power and adhesion.
- Grease resistant and perspiration absorbent properties.
- Removes the shine of talc.
- It has soothing effects on the skin.
- It is used in formulation to adjust fluffiness and control bulk.
- The colour of the kaolin used should be as light as possible.

3. Precipitated Chalk (Calcium Carbonate)

- Reduces the shine of talc and has good covering power.
- It helps to absorb the perfume.
- Grease-resistant and perspiration-absorbent.
- Develops the bloom effect when face powder is applied.
- When this raw material is used in excess, the powder may acquire a dry feel, but moderate usage is most helpful to face powder.

4. Magnesium Carbonate

- It has fine absorbent properties.
- It should be employed in moderate concentrations, since use in excess may result in a drying effect on the skin.

5. Metallic Stearates

- The most important characteristics of zinc and magnesium stearates are their adhesive and waterproofing properties.
- Also possesses a soothing quality.
- Used in moderate amounts 4 to 15%.

6. **Zinc Oxide**
   - Have certain therapeutic properties and help to clear up minor skin disorders.
   - It possesses moderate adhesive properties.
   - To avoid any drying effect and yet allow for sufficient coverage, a formulation may consist of as much as 25%.

7. **Titanium Dioxide**
   - Three to four times better as a covering agent than zinc oxide.
   - It has less adhesion and does not blend well.
   - Used alone or in conjunction with zinc oxide, 10 to 15% titanium dioxide show sufficient covering.

8. **Rice starch**
   - It is an ideal nutrient for bacteria.
   - The bloom and absorbent properties that were contributed by the use of the rice starch are now provided by calcium carbonate and other materials.

9. **Silica and Silicates**
   - Maintains free flowing characteristics.
   - Acts as a Perfume carriers.
   - Silicates such as magnesium trisilicate, have extremely high water-and-oil absorption properties.

II) **Colour**
   - The quantity of Colour required depends to a great degree on the type of base used.

Red	
D and C Red No. 7	Calcium lake
D and C Red No. 9	Barium lake
D and C Red No. 12	Barium lake
D and C Red No. 13	Strontium lake
D and C Red No. 19	Aluminium lake
D and C Red No. 21	Aluminium lake
D and C Red No. 36	Barium lake
Orange	
D and C Orange No. 4	Aluminium lake
D and C Orange No. 17	Barium lake
Yellow	
D and C Yellow No. 5	Aluminium lake

III) Perfume

- Perfume should be non-irritating, stable to mildly alkaline conditions and not undergo oxidation or volatilize too easily.
- The fragrance must be compatible with all of the powder ingredients since problem with rancidity, heterogeneity of odour and discolouration may result from improper odour selection.
- 0.2 -1% is a reasonable perfume rang in a face powder.

Formula of Loose face powder

Light Powder	Medium Powder	Heavy Powder
Talc - 55 gm	Talc - 40 gm	Talc - 40 gm
Kaolin - 15 gm	Kaolin - 12 gm	Kaolin (light) - 10 gm
Calcium carbonate - 8 gm	Calcium carbonate - 10 gm	Calcium carbonate - 8 gm
Zinc oxide - 10 gm	Zinc oxide - 18.0 gm	Zinc oxide - 22.0 gm
Magnesium stearate - 5.0 gm	Titanium dioxide - 10.0 gm	Titanium dioxide - 10.0 gm
Magnesium carbonate - 7.0 gm	Zinc stearate - 5.0 gm	Zinc stearate - 5.0 gm
Colour and perfume - q.s.	Magnesium carbonate - 5.0 gm	Magnesium carbonate - 5.0 gm
	Colour and perfume - q.s.	Colour and perfume - q.s.

2.9.2 Compact Face Powder

It is a dry powder which has been compressed into a cake. The pressure for compaction is very important. The powder must come off easily when rubbed with puff.

Type of binder	Examples
Dry binder	Zn/Mg stearates
Oil binder (water repellant)	Mineral oil, Isopropyl myristate, Lanolin derivatives
Water soluble binder	PVP, CMC, Cellulose, Acacia, Tragacanth
Emulsion binder	Triethanolamine stearates, Glycerol monostearates

Method of Preparation of Compact Face Powder

Compression Method: There are three general procedures,

1. **The Wet Molding Process**
   - The mixture is made paste like with water and cast into molds.
   - The upper surface of the paste is coated with an adhesive and then pressed down by properly shaped metal or glass plates to which the tablets adhered.
   - The tablets are then allowed to dry and are withdrawn from the molds.

2. **The Damp Compressing Method**
   - The mixture is wetted down with a liquid binder and then blended until the proper plasticity of the mass has been attended.
   - The powder is then screened and passed to compression machines, the finished compacts are dried at elevated temperature.

3. **The Dry Compressing Method**
   - The mixtures are milled and the milled powder may moisten with binder, the mixture is then thoroughly blended and the powder is pressed. This method is preferred since very little binding agent is required.

Formulae for Compact face powder

Formula 1	Formula 2
Talc to make : 100 gm	Talc to make : 100 gm
Kaolin : 17. 0 gm	Calcium Carbonate : 10 gm
TiO_2 : 7.0 gm	Zinc Oxide : 5.0 gm
Zinc Stearate : 5.0 gm	Zinc Stearate : 5.0 gm
Colour, Binder and Perfume : q.s.	Colour, Binder and Perfume : q.s.

Evaluation of Face Powder and Compacts

a. **Shade Control**

   The Colour of the powder is checked by:

   1. Spreading the powder out and flattened on a white background.
   2. By applying the powder to the skin.
   3. The Colour of the pressed powder in the correct container is assessed.

   In each case the sample being assessed is compared for shade to the standard.

b. **Dispersion of Colour**

   Colour dispersion is checked by spreading the powder onto a white surface and examining under magnification.

c. **Pay off**

   It is the transfer of powder from the container to the puff. Pay off should be assessed on the skin using the correct applicator.

d. **Pressure Testing**

   Pressure applied to compact powder should be uniform to prevent air pocket and thus breaking or cracking. Uniformity of hardness can be tested by penetrometer. Reading of the hardness is checked at various points of compact tablet to see the uniformity of hardness.

e. **Breakage Test**

This is carried out by dropping the compact tablet of powder on a wooden surface several times from a height of 8 to 10 inches and checking the breakage or clipping of the compact. If the cake is unbroken it is indication of the resistance against travel and normal handling.

f. **Flow Property**

This is very important, particularly for body powders as they should come out easily from the container for easy application. This can be studied by measuring angle of repose of powder product by allowing falling on a plate from a funnel and measuring the height and radius of heap formed.

g. **Particle Size and Abrasiveness**

Particle size can be determined by microscope, sieve analysis or by using sophisticated instrument and techniques. Abrasiveness can be studied by rubbing the powders on a smooth surface and then studying the effect on the surface using microscope.

h. **Moisture Content and Limit for Colour**

This can be estimated by using suitable analytical methods.

2.9.3 Talcum / Body Powder Powders

It consists of mainly talc, with small portion of metallic stearates, precipitated chalk, and magnesium carbonate (light). Talcum/body powders containing antiseptic substances are also used for prickly heat and fungus infections. Zinc oxide acts as a mild astringent and has antiseptic properties.

> Zinc oxide - 5.0 gm
>
> Zinc stearate - 5.0 gm
>
> Chlorhexidine diacetate - 0.3 gm
>
> Light magnesium carbonate - 10.0 gm
>
> Talc to make - 100 gm
>
> Perfume - q.s.

2.10 FACE PACKS AND MASKS

2.10.1 Face Packs

Face packs been used by women from very early time. They are applied in both liquid or paste forms and allowed to dry it. After drying it produces tightening effect on facial skin, produces stimulating sensation of rejuvenation and restores vitality and health of the skin.

Ideal Properties

(1) It should form a smooth paste, free from gritty particles and should have pleasant odour.

(2) When applied should dry out rapidly to form an adherent coating on face. However, coating should be such which can be removed either by peeling off or by gentle washing without causing pain.

(3) It should produce a sensation of tightening.

(4) It should be capable of producing significant cleansing of skin.

(5) It should be non-toxic to skin.

There are five basic types:

1) Wax based formulation
2) Rubber based formulation
3) Hydrocolloid based formulation
4) Vinyl resin based formulation
5) Earth based formulation.

1) Wax Based Formulation

Generally consists of paraffin wax, petroleum jelly, microcrystalline wax etc. Polar materials such as stearyl and cetyl alcohol are also used. Paraffin wax may be replaced by mixture of waxes. These products are solids or liquids and should be melted before application. They are applied with the help of brush. On cooling waxes solidity and a sensation of tightening is felt. It gives moisture proof coating, it causes profuse perspiration, flushes out dirt, impurities, follicular opening in the skin. To facilitate application thixotropy can be impacted by adding bentonite.

Ingredients	Per cent of Total	Role
Paraffin wax	60	Waxes base
Microcrystalline wax	12	
Mineral oil	22	Solvents
Cetyl alcohol	4	
Isopropyl alcohol	0.5	Emollient
Bentonite	1.5	Earth base

2) Rubber Based Formulations (Rubber latex)

It contains latex emulsion, forms continuous, elastic and water impermeable. This interferes with skin perspiration leads to increase in the temperature of applied area, which results in increased blood blow.

Ingredients	Per cent of Total
Latex Emulsion	27
Methyl cellulose	8
Sorbitol	6
Kaolin	4
Borax	1
Water to make	100
Perfume	q.s.

3) Hydrocolloid Based Formulation

They can be formed in the form of high viscous solution or in the form of solid gels, which are required to be melted before application. Feeling of tightness is left behind on shrinking of skin on drying. Various gums used in this formulations are acacia, tragacanth, guar gum, gelatin, CMC, polyvinylpyrolidone etc. Humectants, such as glycerin, propylene glycol; sorbitol solution is used as plasticizers. Viscosity can be varied by changing gum and its concentration.

Hydrocolloid is easy to apply but cleansing action is inferior to face pack which contains adsorbents (kaolin). If rapid drying is required ethyl alcohol can be added. When alcohol is used, only those hydrocolloids should be used which are soluble in hydro alcoholic solution. Small quantity of solid in the form of fine powder can be added which act as opacifier.

Ingredients	Per cent of Total
Gum Tragacanth	2
Glycerin	3
Gelatin	2.5
Zinc Oxide	2
Water to make	100
Preservatives & perfumes	q.s.

2.10.2 Scrubber (Masks)

They are used for their cleansing action but not for tightening effect. They are applied by massaging on skin. Then allowed to remain on skin for about 10-20 minutes and then removed with the help of wet towel or cotton. Grain meal is commonly obtain from one or more grains like oat, barley, wheat, corn etc. Zinc oxide is usually added to almond meal. Preservation is required as grain meal is susceptible to microbial growth.

Ingredients	Per cent of Total
Talc	14
Glycerin	20
Sorbitol (70%)	6
Water to make	100
Almond meal	12
Grain meal	23
Colour, perfume and preservative	q.s.

2.10.3 Manufacture

1) Powder

If the face pack has to be manufactured in the powder form all powder are blended together in blender. The powder mixture is then transferred to filling machine. This may either be filled in bulk containers or in sachet.

2) Paste Mask (Planetary dough mixers)

Here, as they forms heavy compact masses, mixing equipment should have sufficient power so that through mixing and blending is achieved. Wide bowl tops facilitate transfer of bulky material and then they are detached from mixing tank, where semi-finished product is obtain.

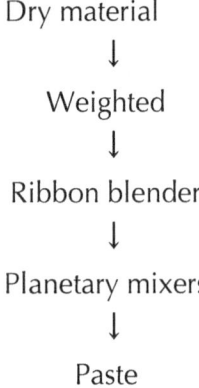

Dry material
↓
Weighted
↓
Ribbon blender
↓
Planetary mixers
↓
Paste

If liquid phase contain humectants and other water soluble ingredient, these may be mixed with water prior to addition to liquid phase. The liquid phase is added in small addition to dry solid in mixer with constant agitation. Initially, the product is very viscous dough, if more addition of liquid is done the viscosity decreases.

Thus, the addition may be made at shorter time intervals. If esters and waxes are added they should be molten before addition. If both fatty materials and water are to be added then they should be heated to almost same temperature and the product is seem to as that of emulsion. If pigment are to be added they should be dispersed in small quantity of solids and then into the powder mixture.

Evaluation parameters are texture, odour, non-grittiness, colour and spread ability.

1) Vinyl Resins Based Formulation

Vinyl resins like polyvinyl alcohol or polyvinyl acetate forms continuous films. Adsorbents are also added.

Ingredients	Per cent of Total	Role
Polyvinyl alcohol	14	Vinyl resin
Propylene glycol	10	Humectants

Contd...

Ingredients	Per cent of Total	Role
Mg-Al Silicate	0.5	Veegum gum
Kaolin	0.7	Adsorbents
Titanium dioxide (TiO_2)	0.3	Adsorbents
Ethyl alcohol	20	Solvent
Water to make	100	Solvent

2) Earths Based Formulation

They are either powder or pastes. They contain a high percentage of solids. Main contents are china clay, colloidal clay, Kaolin, fuller's earth bentonite etc. This is or can be highly contaminated with microorganisms, so needed to be sterilized by heat at near about 40°C.

Water is required to be mixed before use. Mask is formed on drying. Harden the skin and giving a sensation of astringency. Adsorbent clay is added to give cleaning effect. Hydrocolloids may be added to stabilize the suspension of solids. Humectants act as plasticizers. It may also contain astringents, bleaching agents etc.

Oxygenated face masks: It contain peroxides (Mg-peroxide) for oily skin. It is either in powder or paste form and peel of type containing alginates as main ingredient.

Ingredients	Per cent of Total	Role
Kaolin	33	Earth base
Bentonite	6	Earth base
Cetyl alcohol	2	Emollient
Sodium lauryl sulphate	0.1	Surface active agent
Glycerine	12	Humectants
Water to make	100	Vehicle
Perfumes and preservatives	q.s.	

2.11 FACE MAKE-UP

Make-up products include many systems such as lipstick, lip colour, foundations, nail polish, mascara, etc, All these products contain a colouring agent which could be a soluble dye or a pigment (organic or inorganic). Organic pigments are red, yellow, orange and blue lakes. The inorganic pigments comprise titanium dioxide, mica, zinc oxide, talc, iron oxide (red, yellow and black), ultramarines, chromium oxide, etc. Many pigments are modified by surface treatment using amino acids, chitin, lecithin, metal soaps, natural wax, polyacrylates, polyethylene, silicones, etc.

The colour cosmetics comprise foundation, blushers, mascara, eyeliner, eye shadow, lip colour and nail enamel. Their main function is to improve appearance, impart colour, even out skin tones, hide imperfections and produce some protection.

A preservative such as methyl parabens is also included. The surface treated pigments are dispersed either in the oil or aqueous phase. Other additives such as fragrances, vitamins and light diffusers may also be incorporated.

Several anhydrous liquid (or "semi-solid") foundations are also marketed by cosmetic companies. These may be described as cream powders consisting of a high content of pigment/fillers (40-50%), a low HLB wetting agent (such as polysorbate 85), an emollient such as dimethicone combined with liquid fatty alcohols and some esters e.g. octyl palmitate. Some waxes such as stearyl dimethicone or carnauba wax are also included in the formulation.

One of the most important make-up systems is lipsticks which may be simply formulated with a pure fat base having a high gloss and excellent hiding power. However, these simple lipsticks tend to come off the skin too easily. In recent years, there was a great tendency to produce more "permanent" lipsticks which contain hydrophilic solvents such as glycols or tetrahydrofurfuryl alcohol. The raw materials for a lipstick base include: ozokerite (good oil absorbent that also prevents crystallization), micro-crystalline ceresin wax (which is also a good oil absorbent), Vaseline (that forms an impermeable film), bees wax (that increases resistance: to fracture), myristyl myristate (that improves transfer to the skin), cetyl and myristyl lactate (that forms an emulsion with moisture on the lip and are non-sticky), carnauba wax (an oil binder that increases the melting point of the base and gives some surface luster), lanolin derivatives, olyl alcohol and isopropyl myristate. This shows the complex nature of a lipstick base and several modifications of the base can produce some desirable effects that help good marketing of the product.

Mascara and eyeliners are also complex formulations that need to be carefully applied to the eye lashes and edges. Some of the preferred criteria for mascara are good deposition, ease of separation and lash curling. The appearance of the mascara should be as natural as possible. Lash lengthening and thickening are also desirable. The product should also remain for an adequate time and it should also be easily removable. Three types of formulations may be distinguished: anhydrous solvent based suspension, water-in-oil emulsion and oil-in-water emulsion. Water resistance can be achieved by addition of emulsion polymers, e.g. polyvinyl acetate.

Before applying make-up, cleanse your face thoroughly. Then moisten the fingertips with cold water and cool the surface of your face.

Step One: The Foundation

The first step in the make-up process is the application of the correct foundation base colour. The foundation turns the face into a blank mask upon which facial features are accentuated and shaped with makeup. There are two types of foundation: cream makeup and cake (pancake) makeup. Cream is preferred because of its ease of blending, and it works well with soft liners. Cream base is usually applied directly with the fingers after a few spots have been dabbed on the face and neck. In addition, pancake makeup is very difficult to mix and does not blend well with soft liners.

Step Two: Shadows and Highlights

The application of shadow and highlight is really the most important aspect of modeling the face. Highlighting and shadowing are used for three purposes:

1. to bring out features
2. to correct features
3. to change features to indicate age, character, or physical impairments

Step Three: Rouge and Lipstick

Apply moist rouge to cheeks and lips next. The manner in which you apply the rouge will vary according to the shape of your face. Lipstick may be applied with the little finger if the natural lip line is followed. If the shape of the lips is to be altered or emphasized, however, a lipstick brush should be used. The lips should be blocked out by covering the outer edges with the foundation when it is applied.

Step Four: Eyes and Eyebrows

Applying makeup to the eyes and brows is the next step. The eyes and the mouth are the most expressive features of the face, and the brows give the greatest character to the eyes. The purpose of eye shadow is to beautify the eyes, to make them seem larger, and to indicate character. Apply eye shadow to the upper lids only, beginning with a heavy application in the crease and fading out, blending the colour over the eyelid. The choice of colour is determined by the colour of hair and costume, the personality. Another technique that enlarges and accents the eyes is eye lining. Brown or black lining colour may be used, but black is acceptable. In straight parts, the eyebrows should frame the eyes rather than attract attention. Brown or black pencil may be used to shape the brows.

Step Five: Powdering

The most important step in the application of cream makeup is applying powder. Use powder that is translucent or a shade that is one tone lighter than the foundation. Powder, when properly applied, sets the makeup, softens the lines and colours, and gives a matte finish, which removes the shine of the makeup under lights. Powder must be squeezed into the puff and the excess shaken off. Then it should be pressed into the makeup thoroughly but gently. Be very careful not to rub or smear the makeup. An even coat of powder holds the makeup in place and prevents it from running under lights.

Step Six: Finishing Touches

After the powder, you may apply the finishing touches. If the powder dulled the cheeks, dry rouge may be used to restore the colour, but be sure no lines or spots of rouge are visible.

2.12 COLOURED MAKE-UP PREPARATIONS

2.12.1 Lipsticks

The practice of applying colour to cheecks and lips is very old. Today lipstick is one of the most widely used cosmetics by women. Lipsticks are basically dispersion of colouring matter in a base consisting of suitable of oils, fats and waxes suitably perfumed and flavoured, moulded in the form of stick and enclosed in a case.

Applications of Lipstick

1] To impart an attractive colour.

2] To give glossy and moist appearance to lips.

3] Accentuating good points of lips.

4] Disguising the defects.

5] To prevent cracking and chapping of lips.

A lipstick should have the following characteristics:

1] It should cover the lips adequately with some glass and last for long time.

2] It should make the lips soft.

3] The film must adhere firmly to lips without being brittle and tacky.

4] It should have a good degree of indelibility.

5] It should have high retention of colour intensity without any change in shade.

6] It should be completely free from grittiness and be non-drying.

7] It should be non-irritating to skin of lips.

8] It should have a desirable degree of plasticity.

9] It should have a pleasant odour and flavour.

Lipsticks should also have the following storage characteristics :

1] A smooth and shiny appearance.

2] Freedom from bloom or sweating.

3] Retain plasticity without any tendency to dry out or crumble.

4] A suitable degree of firmness during reasonable variation of climate temperature.

Formulation

The lipstick mainly contains a colour material dispersed and suspended in a suitable base made by blending oils and waxes in various proportion to yield desired melting point and viscosity. The temperature of human body varies between 36°C to 38°C with lips having the higher side. The base of lipstick must have a melting point appreciably higher than this, between 55°C to 75°C preferably about 62°C for the product to withstand exposure to hot climates.

Other Lipstick Formulations

Transparent Lipsticks

➤ Transparent lipsticks do not contain any insoluble opaque pigment or lakes but instead uses soluble or solubilized dyes. This allow light to shine through them giving it a sparkle. The staining action of these dyes is enhanced by using a suitable solvent such as monoalkylamide of mixed fatty acid or dipropylene glycol.

➤ Water soluble dyes may be used for additional colour instead of oil soluble dyes.

➤ For moulding purposes polyamide resins (solid) having molecular weight ranging from 2000-10,000 are blended with liquid polyamide resins having molecular weight ranging from 600-800.

➤ To ensure that the lipstick made up of resins is not brittle, a softening agent likes lower aliphatic alcohols in conjugation with other polyamide solvent such as fatty acid esters is added.

Liquid Lipsticks

➤ Liquid lipsticks have been developed with an object of providing more permanent film than that can be obtained with conventional lipsticks.

➤ Liquid lipsticks consist of an alcoholic solution of alcohol soluble dyes, a film former, plasticizer etc.

➤ The solvent employed is ethyl alcohol or isopropyl alcohol.

➤ The film former includes ethyl cellulose, polyvinyl alcohols and polyvinyl acetate.

➤ Plasticizers such as triethyl citrate, dioctyl acetate, methyl acetate or polyethylene glycols.

➤ The dye stuffs employed are alcohol soluble halogenated fluorescein and other alcohol soluble dyes.

Lip Salves/Balm

➤ These are used to protect lip from drying during winter season.

➤ Thus, there is a requirement that the lip salve should form a flexible, adherent, moisture resistant film on the lips and there is no need of staining dye and dye solvent.

➤ The base can be made largely from mineral oil, jelly and waxes.

➤ It is necessary to include a more hydrophilic material to promote adherence, perfume blending and general properties.

➤ In some cases a small amount of an antiseptic may be included.

Lip Gloss

➤ Lip gloss is decorated salves.

➤ These are either used alone or to cover a lipstick application.

➤ They may be available in solid, semisolid or liquid form.

➤ They are prepared with or without colorants.

➤ Sometimes, these contain pearl pigments to produce a transparent shine on the lip as well as gloss.

Rouge/Blush

> ➤ Rouge/Blush is a cosmetic typically used by women to redden the cheeks, to provide a more youthful appearance and to emphasize the cheek bones.

The basic raw materials required for formulating lipsticks can be classified as:

1] Wax mixture

2] Oil mixture

3] Bromo mixture

4] Colours

5] Preservatives, fragrances, surfactants and other additives.

1] Waxes

Gloss and hardness of lipsticks are largely dependent on characteristics and quantity of waxes used. So, the composition of wax mixture is of prime importance. Best characteristics can be obtained by using a mixture of waxes of different melting point and adjusting final melting point by incorporating a sufficient amount of high melting point wax. Various waxy materials used in lipsticks are:

Sr. No.	Name of The Ingredient	Melting Range	Per cent Used	Remark
1.	Hard paraffin	50-57	1-5	Improves gloss
2.	Ceresin wax	60-75	5-20	Increases melting point
3.	Ozokerite wax	60-80	1-10	Imparts short fibred texture
4.	Candilella wax	65-69	5-10	Gives smooth and glossy appearance
5.	White bees wax	62-64	5-20	Binds oil and high melting waxes
6.	Carnauba wax	81-86	1-3	Imparts rigidity hardness
7.	Cetyl alcohol	45-50	2-3	Gives emollient properties
8.	Cestosteryl alcohol	43	2-3	Gives emollient properties
9.	Spermaceti wax	42-50	5-15	Blender
10.	Lanolin	36-42	5-15	Blender
11.	Soft paraffin	38-56	1-5	As a lubricant and improves spreading properties.

2] Oils

The oil mixture is required to blend properly with the waxes to provide a suitable film on the applied skin. It also acts as solvent for eosin dye stuffs or as dispersing agent for insoluble pigments. Ideal mixture is one which enables the product to spread easily and produces a thin film with good covering powder.

a) Castor oil

1] It is mainly used because of its good qualities.

2] A refined grade castor oil is of good colour, odourless and tasteless.

3] It is a very good plasticizing agent.

4] An antioxidant is added to castor oil against rancidification.

5] High viscosity of castor oil makes the dispersion of pigments long stable during the mixing and moulding stages of manufacturing.

6] Normally, about 40-50% castor oil is used.

b) Tetrahydrofurfuryl alcohol and its esters

Alcohols and its esters like acetate, stearates, ricinoleate are also used in lipstick preparation. The acetate has very good solvent property for eosin dye. But the volatile property of solvent can lead to smudging of the outline by evaporation from hotter inner surface and deposition on the cooler edges. Acetate has an unpleasant taste and odour. But stearates and ricinoleate are good and non-volatile but their solvent property is little less.

c) Fatty acid alkaylamides

1] They are non-volatile and have no unpleasant taste or odour.

2] They increases stability of lipstick but do not have emollient action.

3] They help in dispersing the pigments.

d) Paraffin Oil

1] It is used not more than 5% to give glossy appearance after application.

2] In higher proportion, the oil will come off the lips and run around lips.

3] Also act as lubricant to facilitate removal of sticks from moulds.

3] Bromo Mixture

The bromo mixture is essentially, a solution of the staining dyestuff in a fatty material to unable the dyestuff to remain either wholly or partially in solution. This is the portion of product which imparts an indelible stain as distinct from opaque film of colour given by insoluble pigments. The dyestuff of bromo mixture, known as bromo acids, consists of fluorescein; halogenated fluorescein and related water insoluble dyes. Bromo acid colours can be classified into two groups:

➤ Which are red and gives a red or reddish – blue stain.

➤ Which are orange, red and give pink to yellowish – pink stain.

Other solvents used are tetrahydrofurfuryl alcohol and esters like acetate, stearates glycerol derivatives like glyceryl mono stearates and glyceryl monolaurate. Propylene glycol and polyethylene glycol are used as suitable colour solvents.

4] Colours

The colour of lipstick is most important from commercial and appealing point of view. Colour is imported to the lips in two ways:

i) By staining the skin with solution of dyestuff which can penetrate the outer layer of lip skin.

ii) By covering the lips with a coloured layer which serves to hide any skin roughness and give a smooth appearance.

a) Staining dyes

Most widely used staining dyes are fluorescein, eosin and often halogenated fluorescein. Fluorescein and its derivatives produce sensitization or photosensitization leading to cheilitis (inflammation of red portion of the lips).

Water solubility character possess problem for formulation. But when water soluble dyes are converted to free sulpho acid form, they become insoluble, lipophilic and suitable for use as staining dyes.

b) Insoluble dyestuff and lake colours

These are the colouring agent which covers the thin layer over the lips. They consists of calcium, barium, aluminium and strontium lakes. Calcium and barium lakes prepared from azo type dyestuff, are also used. These are called lake toners.

5] Perfumes, Preservatives and Additives

Preservatives: Propyl parahydroxy benzoate (0.1%) commonly used as a preservative. Higher concentration may cause burning sensation which may trigger off an eosin allergic reaction.

Flavours: They should not contain an ingredient which is irritating or toxic. They should have good test and should be able to mask fatty odour of base.

Antioxidant: Antioxidants are added to prevent rancidity on storage. For example, BHT, BHA, propyl gallate or combination is used to impart synergism.

Ingredients	Per cent of total	Function
Phase A		
Bees wax	12.5	Thickener
Carnauba wax	7.5	Thickener/emollient
Coconut oil	8	Emollient
Phase B		
Jojoba oil	20	Emollient
Castor oil	43	Emollient
Tocopherol	4	Antioxidant
Phase C		
TiO_2	0.2	Colour base
Food flavoring	0.3	Flavour

Method

1. Add Phase A into a glass beaker and heat to 68°C, until the wax is melted.
2. Remove from the heat.
3. Add Phase B (liquid ingredients) and stir until blended. Reheat gently if required.
4. Add Phase C (pre-blended colour ingredients) and stir until uniform.
5. Fill the mixture while still liquid into lipstick tubes.
6. As soon as the liquid has become solid, the lipstick is ready to use.

Ingredients	Per cent of Total	Role
Castor oil	20	Dispersing agent
Liquid paraffin	15	Dispersing agent
Bees wax	20	Stiffening agent
Paraffin wax	10	Base
Ceresin wax	10	Colouring agent
Candelilla wax	10	Glossy appearance

1) Weigh and melt bees wax, paraffin wax, candelilla wax with the decreasing order of their melting point.
2) Add castor oil and liquid paraffin to the molten mass with stirring which are premixed.
3) Pour the molten mass in the lipstick mould, scrap overfill.

Ingredients	Per cent of Total
Castor oil	30
Mineral oil	3.0
Bess wax	18.0
Lanoline	5
Cetyl alcohol	2.0
Isopropyl myristate	2.0
Ozokerite wax	10
Carnauba wax	3.0
Propylene glycol	10
Propylene glycol mono-myristate	5.0
Lake colours	8.0
Bromoacids	2.0
Perfume, preservatives and antioxidant	q.s.

Ingredients	Per cent of Total
Castor oil	40
Bees wax	5
Lanolin	2.5
Isopropyl myristate	2.5
Ozokerite wax	5
Carnauba wax	3
Candelilla wax	7
Propylene glycol	5
Glyceryl monostearate	4
Acetylated mono glyceride (solid)	6
Acetylated mono glyceride (liquid)	3
Lake colours	15
Bromoacids	2
Perfume, preservative and antioxidant	q.s.

Ingredients	Per cent of Total
Castor oil	43
Isopropyl linoleate	1.5
Isopropyl myristate	2.5
Lanolin	2
Acetylated Mono Glyceride (solid)	6
Acetylated mono glyceride (liquid)	3
Bees wax	7
Candelilla wax	8
Ozokerite wax	6
Carnauba wax	5
Propylene glycol	4
Propylene glycol mono myristate	10
Bromoacids	2
Perfume, preservative and antioxidant	q.s.

Manufacture

1] Colour Dispersion

➢ For preparing smooth lipstick, agglomerates of color pigments must be broken down, so those free particles are surrounded by oil.

➢ To break the agglomerates of pigments effectively, a rubbing or shearing force of considerable magnitude should be applied. This can be achieved with a variety of mills. For example, Ball mill, roller mill and colloidal mill etc.

➢ If some suitable solvent is used for preparing solution of bromo acids, it is prepared first and set aside.

➢ Lake colours are first dispersed in a suitable quantity of oil to make a paste.

➢ This paste is passed through triple roller mill till, so that it is free from agglomerates of colour partials.

➢ If formula contains TiO_2 it is treated in the same way as that of lake colours before mixing into the colour mix.

➢ Low melting point waxes are melted next and added to colour mix.

➢ This mixture is passed through mill until it becomes perfectly smooth.

➢ Preservatives and anti-oxidant are dissolved in remaining oil and added to colour mixture.

➢ High melting point waxes are melted last and added to colour mix.

2] Mixing

➢ For batch processing of lipstick, the equipment that is used is jacketed kettle made of inert material like Al, stainless steel (SS), tinned copper.

➢ A kettle is having hemispherical bottom, that is easiest to empty and can be cleaned easily.

➢ The kettle is heated either with steam or water. High melting point waxes are then added to colour mix and stirred slowly.

➢ Overheating should be avoided. Rapid stirring should also be avoided as it may lead to air entrapment which may create problem in blending. Perfume is added.

➢ Next the molten mixture is strained through fine mesh screen and transferred to moulds or storage containers.

➢ If this material is to be stored for longer period, storage containers should be made up of inert material and should be air tight.

3] Moulding

➢ For moulding operation brass and aluminium moulds are used.

➢ Cleaved two halves of moulds are joined together with clamps.

➢ Molten lipstick mixture is run on to the seat of the mould. Excess material is run into the space over cavities so that central holes or wells are not formed due to shrinkage on congealing.

➢ The moulds are allowed to stand without movement until the material undergoes solidification.

➢ The extra material is scrapped off and moulds are transferred to chilled metallic plates. Over cooling should be avoided, otherwise the moulds has to be heated before refilling. As soon as the lipsticks are firm enough to handle, moulds are unclamped and they are pushed out with the help of finger.

4] Flaming

➢ The sticks are inserted in lipstick containers which are available in a variety of types.

➢ After inserting sticks into the containers free end of sticks is reheated for a very short time.

➢ This makes the surface of stick smooth and glossy.

➢ This process is usually done by passing lipstick through gas flame.

➢ The lipstick is rotated so that entire surface is exposed to heat.

Evaluation of Lipsticks

Closed Prophetic Test

Select 200 normal subjects.

The lipstick formulation is applied to them for 1-5 days depending on judgment of the investigator

Examine the patch sites and observations are made

Subjects are observed for 3 more days for development of any late reaction

After 7-10 days, patches are again applied to same area of those subject who did not show reactions to the test

Along with test lipstick formulation a well established lipstick in market should be used as a control

If results of patch test and actual user test are favorable, an extensive user test on additional 800 subjects should be carried out before lipstick is put on the market.

Quality Control of Ingredients and Bulk Finished Product

The material used in lipstick should be subjected to strict control to ascertain uniformity in all significant properties. Waxes can be evaluated for their crystal structure and softening point. Pigments can be evaluated for their fineness. Oils can be evaluated for Viscosity. As lipsticks should not contain more than 100 micro-organisms per gram raw material should also be subjected for microbiological examination.

In manufactured lipsticks, following in-process checks can be carried out.

1. Colour match
2. Texture
3. Softening point

1. Colour Match

It is important that, every time, for a particular shade the same shade is produced as that standard shade therefore colour match should be done.

2. Texture

The texture should not be gritty, the product should be smooth.

3. Softening point

It gives an indication whether lipstick will be able to withstand variations in climate temperature or not. Since, India is a tropical country and temperature in some regions goes as high as 48°C, the softening point of lipstick should be sufficiently high so that lipstick can withstand high temperature.

According to IS, lipstick should have softening point not less than 55°C. In case of new product both shelves testing as well as oven testing should be carried out to ensure that the product will be able to withstand climatic variations in temperatures.

Breaking Point Test

To carry out this test, the lipstick is held horizontally in a socket fitting over about ½ inch of its base and weight is applied at a measured distance from the edge of support. The weight applied is increased every 30 seconds by predetermined increments until the lipstick breaks. On a given lot, at least four readings should be made. Test should be carried out at 25-30°C.

Ageing Stability

It can be performed by storing the lipsticks in oven at 40°C and by making periodic observation of oil bleed, crystallization of waxes on surface and applicability.

Perfume Stability

It can be performed by storing lipstick in an oven at 40°C and making periodic comparison of perfume with fresh lipstick.

Oxidative Stability

It can be performed by determining peroxide value, after lipstick has been exposed to O_2 under given conditions.

2.13 SUNTAN AND SUNSCREEN PREPARATION

When UV light penetrates skin, it can interact with biological molecules, give up its energy and cause transient and/or permanent changes in those biological molecules. Any molecule which is capable of absorbing light is referred to as a chromophore and biological systems such as human skin contain many potential chromophores. Exactly which chromophores actually absorb light, and how this manifests itself as skin damage, is dependent upon both the energy of the incident light and its depth of penetration into skin. UVA is often over-simplistically identified as UV-'A' for ageing. This is because its long term effects on the dermal layers of human skin manifest themselves as visual wrinkling and ageing of the skin. However, UVA is also capable of generating both immediate skin pigmentation and delayed pigmentation, the latter being the tanning response. UVA also contributes approximately 15% of the sunburn reaction which occurs as a result of overexposure to summer sunshine. UVB penetrates only as far as the basal cell layer and possibly into the upper margins of the dermis. Most adverse effects of UVB light on skin arise from the absorption of UVB by chromophores in the living and actively dividing cells of the lower epidermis and basal cell layer, i.e. the keratinocytes, melanocytes and Langerhans' cells. UVA, on the other hand, will penetrate far deeper into the skin, penetrating through the epidermis and deep into the dermis where it can initiate photochemical reactions within structural components of the skin such as collagen and elastin. Consequently, it can be seen that the epidermis with its basal cell layer is invaded by both UVB and UVA wavelengths, whilst the dermis suffers primarily from UVA aggression. The cells of the epidermis and the basal cell layer contains many constituents which may act as UVB chromophores. However, the major epidermal chromophore is deoxyribonucleic acid (DNA). The high energy contained within a photon of UVB light is sufficient to induce permanent structural changes in DNA and, in doing so, will disrupt the genetic coding of individual cells. In most cases, this damage is corrected by cellular 'repair' mechanisms, but occasionally 'repair' is not 100% accurate or complete and this may ultimately lead to the degenerative process of malignancy. Whilst the subject of malignant melanomas, carcinomas and solar keratoses is beyond the scope of this chapter, it is worth noting that epidemiological evidence links high UVB exposure (i.e. lower latitudes) and low natural skin pigmentation, with increased incidence of melanoma.

Skin Type and Choice of Sunscreens

A sunscreen product protects different individuals to the different extent. This depends on individual skin type. Depending on skin type and tanning history individuals can be classified as follows:

- Always burns easily and never tans (i.e. sensitive)
- Always burns and tans minimally (i.e. sensitive)
- Burns moderately and tans gradually to a shade of light brown (i.e. normal)
- Burns minimally and always tans well (i.e. normal)
- Barely burns and tans profusely-skin becomes dark brown (i.e. insensitive)
- Never burns and skin becomes deeply pigmented (i.e. insensitive)

Sun Protecting Factor (SPF)

Sun protecting factor (SPF) is defined as relative effectiveness of sunscreen agents to protect the skin. Thus, numerically identifying the efficacy of various sunscreen products and to provide information for consumer about the products suitable for particular types of skin.

2.13.1 Definition

SPF has been defined as the ratio between the UV exposure required to produce a minimally perceptible erythema on protected skin and the exposure that will produce the same erythema on unprotected skin.

$$SPF\ value = MED\ (PS)\ /MED\ (US)$$

where,

MED (PS) = Minimum Erythemal Dose for Protected Skin after the application of 2 mg/ cm or 2 ul/cm^2 of the final formulation of the sunscreen product.

MED (US) = Minimum Erythemal Dose for Unprotected Skin i.e. skin to which no sunscreen product has been applied.

If larger the SPF, the greater will be the protection. The rating numbers to range from 2 – 8. A product having a rating of 8 would thus provide the maximum protection to individuals who always burn easily and never tan (i.e. sensitive). The product having rating of 2 would be suitable for individuals who rarely burn but tan profusely (i.e. insensitive).

Skin Type	SPF
I	8 or more
II	6-7
III	4-5
IV	2-3
V	2
VI	Non-indicated

As mentioned above, a classification system for sun screening product comprises of five Product Category Destinations (PCD). These are

PCD 1	Minimal sun protection product	Such product provides a SPF value of 2-4. It provides least protection but permits sun tanning
PCD 2	Moderate sun protection product	Such product provides a SPF value of 4-6. It provides moderate protection from sun-burning but permits some tanning.
PCD 3	Extra sun protection product	Such product provides a SPF value of 6-8. It provides extra protection from sun- burning but permits some tanning.

| PCD 4 | Maximal sun protection product | Such product provides a SPF value of 8-15. It provides maximal protection from sun burn and permits little or no sun tanning. |
| PCD5 | Ultra sun protection product | Such product provides a SPF value of 15 or more. It provides greater protection from sun burns and no sun tanning. |

Conditions like elevated heat and humidity, sweating, swimming may lower SPF value. Sensitive individuals should use products in ultra protection category i.e. products having SPF value of 15 or more.

2.13.2 Ideal Properties of Sunscreening Agents

➢ It should absorb erythmogenic radiations in the range of 290-320 nm without its breakdown.
➢ It should allow full transmission of radiations 300-400 nm for tanning effect.
➢ It should resist to water and perspiration. It should be non-volatile in nature.
➢ It should have suitable solubility character.
➢ It should be odourless /mild odour, non-toxic, non-irritant, non-sensitizing.
➢ It should effective and stable for several hours.

2.13.3 Effective Sunscreen

- **p-Aminobenzoic acid (PABA) and its derivatives:** 2-ethylhexyl-p-dimethyl aminobenzoate (Octyldimethyl PABA) at allowable levels upto 8.0%.
- **Cinnamate:** 2-ethylhexyl-p-methoxycinnamate (Octylmethoxy cinnamate) at levels upto 10%.
- **Salicylates:** Octyl salicylate can be used at levels up to 5%. Its overall protective effect, however, is poor, its absorbance being far less than PABA or cinnamate derivatives of equivalent concentration. It is often used as a synergist with other sunscreens since it aids their solubility. Homomenthyl salicylate (homosalate) has similar characteristics but may be used at levels upto 10%.
- **Anthranilates:** Menthyl anthranilate can be used upto 5% concentration.
- **Camphor derivatives:** 3-(4-Methylbenzylidene) camphor is becoming much more widely used.
- **Benzophenones:** 2-Hydroxy-4-methoxy-benzophenone (benzophenone-3 or oxybenzone) is widely used at upto 10% concentration.
- **Dibenzoylmethanes:** Octocrylene.

Formulation

1. Product, package and closure should be convenient for use.
2. It should present in effective concentration.
3. Sunscreen and vehicle should be compatible with each other.
4. Choice of lipids and hydrophilic materials based on requirements of degree of greasiness or wetness.

Alcoholic Suntan Lotion

Ingredients	Per cent of Total
Glyceryl p-amino benzoate	3
Polyethylene glycol ricinoleate	8
Glycerin	10
Alcohol	60
Water to make	100
Perfume & colour	q.s.

Aqueous Suntan Lotion with Thickener

Ingredients	Per cent of Total
Glyceryl p-amino benzoate	3
Glycerin	5
Alcohol	10
Methyl cellulose	0.5
Water to make	100
Perfume	q.s.

Clear suntan lotion

Ingredients	Per cent of Total
Isobutyl p- amino benzoate	5
Tween 20	10
Alcohol	45
Water to make	100
Perfume	q.s.

Suntan Cream

Ingredients	Per cent of Total
Stearic acid	18
Cetyl alcohol	0.5
Menthyl anthranilate	5
NaOH	0.5
Glycerin	10
Water to make	100
Perfume	q.s.

Sunscreen Ointment

Ingredients	Per cent of Total
Homomenthyl salicylate	5
Ceresin	14
Groundnut oil	81
Prefume, colour and antioxidants	q.s.

Light Scattering Sunscreen

Ingredients	Per cent of Total
Calamine	15
Petroleum Jelly	38
Lanolin	12
Water to make	100
Perfume	q.s.

Some Palliative Preparations are,

Ingredients	Per cent of Total
Zinc oxide	15
Talc	12
Bentonite	7
Propylene glycol	6
Water to make	100

Ingredients	Per cent of Total
Mineral oil	10
Lanolin	2
Triethanolamine oleate	4
Propylene glycol	3
Water to make	100

2.13.4 Manufacture

Sun screening agents can be incorporated in a variety of cosmetics e.g. lotions, cream, ointments. General method of manufacturising of these formulations can be applied for sunscreens.

CHAPTER 3...

SHAVING PREPARATIONS

INTRODUCTION

The outer layer of the hair is known as cuticle. Cuticle is hard and its hardness is reduced by a hair softening agents. This hair softening is the primary aim of shaving preparations.

Ideal Properties of Shaving Preparations:

- It must be non-irritating to skin.
- It must retain moisture during the period it remains on the face.
- It must soften the beard so that the hair is cut easily.
- It should provide sufficient lubricity so that razor glides along the face.
- It should have sufficient viscosity to hold individual hair erect so that it could be cut close to the surface of the skin.
- It should be stable over a wide range of temperature.
- It should be non-corrosive to the containers in which it is packed.
- If it is to be used with a brush, it should be able to develop high lather rapidly.

3.1 SHAVING SOAPS

Potassium stearates give quicker and stable lather than sodium stearates. But potassium soap is softer, so certain amount of sodium soaps should be added. For stick formulation stearic acid and coconut fatty acid may be saponified with KOH and NaOH. These are available as bar, stick or cup formulation.

Ingredients	Per cent of Total
Stearic acid	48
Coconut fatty acid	15
KOH	20
NaOH	4
Water to make	100

Super fatting agents like monodecyl, dodecyl, tetradecyl ethers of di-glycerol amines can be added. Addition of talc (10-15%) increases persistence of lather. Pilomotor agents cause contraction of hair follicle muscle projecting hair fibre out.

Solid shaving soap can be made in crutcher using a mixture of sodium and potassium hydroxide. In this method, all glycerin that is produced from fats is used in the finished cake. The product has shiny or sticky feel. Glycerin more than 10% should not be produced in the soap formed.

Second method is to use kettle-made boiled soda soap. Soda soap and potassium stearates are added to a crutcher. In this method glycerin is avoided.

In another method, requisite amount of tallow is saponified with potassium hydroxide in the crutcher. To this is added soda soap. Any excess alkali is neutralized with stearic acid. For shaving stick or shaving bowl soap, it is advantageous to use plodder of great packing powder.

3.2 LATHER SHAVING CREAM

Lather creams are mixture of soap in glycerin with water. A good lather cream should have,

- Should produce rich lather.
- Non- irritant and not be astringent.
- Have good wetting property.
- Smooth, soft and free of lumps.
- Should adhere to both face and brush at same time should rinse easily.
- Should retain consistency at different storage conditions.

Properties of Lather Shaving Cream

- Ease of transfer of cream to the face.
- Ease of spreading.
- Wetting property of foam, its texture, rigidity, rheology and stability.
- Closeness of shave.
- Gliding property for ease of shaving.
- Ease with which lather and debris can be removed from razor.
- Compatibility and acceptance of perfume.
- Compatibility with container.

Formulation

i) Lather shaving creams are dispersions of soaps in glycerin and water. It contains 30-50% soaps. For improving lather, coconut fatty acid can be used. Ratio of 75% stearic acid and 25% coconut oil gives satisfactory results. Mixture of KOH and NaOH should be used to saponify oils.

ii) KOH and NaOH in ratio of 5 : 1 with 3-5% free acid gives good plasticity to product.

iii) Humectants prevents premature drying of the cream and makes them softer, for example: glycerin, propylene glycol, sorbitol solution, etc.

iv) Emollient like lanolin, cetyl alcohol, mineral oil, fatty acid esters should be used up to 1%.

v) Super fatting agents (stearic acid, coconut oil, vegetable oil, boric acid etc.), neutralize excess alkali and stabilizes cream and leather.

vi) Other additives are synthetic surfactants i.e. foam stabilizer, cooling agents, antibacterial etc.

Ingredients	Per cent of Total
Stearic acid	28
Coconut oil	12
Palm oil	5 (Super fatting agents)
KOH	6.5
NaOH	1.5
Glycerin	10
Water to make	100
Perfumes and preservatives	q.s.

Ingredients	Per cent of Total
Stearic acid	25
Coconut oil	10
Myristic acid	10
KOH	2.5
NaOH	0.5
Glycerin	5
Water to make	100
Perfumes and preservatives	q.s.

vii) Higher percentage of oil should be avoided, as it is irritating to sensitive skin.

viii) Temperature fluctuation causes changes in the texture of lather cream, as temperature increases viscosity increases i.e., gel-like consistency and as temperature decreases cream becomes hard and difficult to apply. These variation can reduced by adding 0.5% borax. Sodium silicate (1-1.5%) reduces corrosion of metallic tubes.

Manufacture of Lather Shaving Cream

1) Oil/fats are melted, filtered and saponified with NaOH and part of KOH into glycerin.
2) Add remaining KOH in water and mix.
3) Add melted stearic acid continuously with slow stirring.
4) Add superfatting agent e.g. Boric acid, lanolin; additional stearic acid.
5) Discontinue heating and continue stirring while cream cools.
6) When temperature drops i.e. 40-45°C, add perfume.
7) Stand cream for 3-4 weeks and pack.
8) Avoid air entrapment.

Quality Control during Manufacturing

1) **Content of free fatty acid**: It should be determined as it influences the stability of cream at high temperature.
2) **Free alkalinity Test:** Dissolve one gm in 100 ml rectified spirit, should not give colour with phenolphthalein.
3) **Test for suitability of Stearic acid**: Good quality of stearic acid should be used. To test suitability of stearic acid, add an excess of strong KOH solution to stearic acid, if resulting soap is coloured (brown to yellow) it is not suitable.

3.3 BRUSHLESS SHAVING CREAM

This preparation does not required brush for applying. The cream is applied and spread with finger. General formula is as follows:

Ingredients	Per cent
Stearic acid	10-20
Mineral oil	2-12.0
Alkali	0.5-2
Lanolin	0-5
Gums	0-0.5
Water	100
Perfumes and preservatives	q.s.

Formulation

It is an oil/water emulsion. Lanolin can be added in higher proportion. Gum (karaya) can be used. Also synthetic gums like MC, PVP and Sodium CMC can be used.

Ingredients	Per cent of Total
Stearic acid	15
Mineral oil	15
Spermaceti	2
Dilute solution of ammonia	2
Glycerin	5
Water to make	100
Perfumes and Preservatives	q.s

Ingredients	Per cent of Total
Stearic acid	6
Mineral oil	1
GMS	10
Glycerin	4
Water to make	100
Perfumes and Preservatives	q.s.

Manufacturing

1) Add water soluble ingredient in water at 65-70°C.
2) Prepare oil/fat phase at same temperature.
3) Add aqueous phase to oil phase at same temperature.
4) Stir to get emulsification.
5) Cool to 45°C, add perfume.
6) Allow cream to mature for a week.
7) Fill in collapsible tubes/ Jars.

3.4 CLASSIFICATION OF SHAVING PREPARATIONS

- Wet shaving preparation
- Dry shaving preparation
- After shave preparation

3.4.1 Wet Shaving Preparations

The main functional requirements of a wet shaving preparation are

➢ To soften the beard.
➢ To lubricate the passage of the razor over the face.
➢ To support the beard hair.

A shaving preparation irrespective of its physical form must have the following properties,

- It must be non-irritating to the skin.
- It must retain moisture during the period it remains on the face. It must soften beard so that the hair are cut easily.
- It should provide sufficient lubricity so that razor glides along the face.
- It should have sufficient viscosity to hold individual hair erect so that it could be cut close to the surface of skin.
- Stable over wide range of temperature.
- Non-corrosive to the containers in which it is packed.
- Be able to be washed down the drain without creating clogging problems.
- If it is to be used with a brush, it should be able to develop high lather rapidly.

3.4.2 Dry Shaving Preparation

Pre-Electric Shave Preparation

These are designed for dry skin. In liquid form these are based on alcohol as it takes up moisture and dries up quickly. In powder form these are based on talc (also available in aerosol form). These preparations may not increase the quality of shave but may assist in reducing skin damage.

Pre-electric shave lotion contains comparatively high percentage of alcohol. Alcohol besides drying up quickly also causes contraction of erector pili muscles. This action causes the hair to stand out more and thus facilitate cutting.

Antibacterial oily material (to lubricate the hair with thin film oil which acts as cutting lubricant) can also be added. Electric shave powders consists mainly of talc and metallic stearates.

Ingredients	% of Total
Alcohol	90
Isopropyl myristate	10
Perfume	q.s.

3.4.3 After Shave Preparation

The purpose of an after shave preparation is to relieve the slight irritation or "after glow" and confers a pleasant feeling of comforts and well being after shaving. The preparation should be antiseptic and free of bacterial infections.

1) After Shave Lotion

An after shave lotion is a clear aqueous ethyl alcohol (50-70%) solution containing a perfume. Non-ionic surfactant with HLB number in a range 15-18 is the most effective solubilizers. Humectants and emollients like glycerol sorbitol, propylene glycol help to maintain water content of skin. The evaporation of alcoholic solution results cooling.

Ingredients	Per cent of Total
Ethyl alcohol (Denatured)	60
Propylene glycol	03
Water to make	100
Perfume	q.s.

2) After Shave Powder

Main purpose is to alleviate any discomfort product by shaving and leave face cool and refreshed and to cover minor skin defects.

Lather Shaving Stick

These are prepared from a mixture containing 80% of fatty acid soaps, 5-10% glycerol and 8-10% of water. After mixing the composition is chipped, dried and milled with any other components required such as perfumes, colour or an opacifier. The soap flakes are packed to the desired shape using a soap plodder.

Brushless Shaving Stick

Brushless shaving stick can be applied directly to the face. The continuous thin smear left on wetted skin provides an adequate lubrication for the shaving operation. The stick is composed of fatty or waxy materials (having hydrophilic properties imparted by a suitable emulsifier.) Pigment, dyestuff or opacifier is also incorporated.

Aerosol Shaving Lather / Foams

These are o/w emulsions. Propellants droplets liquefied under pressure from a substantial part of oil phase in such preparations. When the preparations are discharged to the atmosphere, droplets of propellants vaporize producing vapour bubbles surrounded by aqueous surfactant phase.

Guidelines for Formulation

Saturated fatty acid (7-9%) (C_{12} – C_{18}) are main components. Alkalies like TEA, KOH mixture of these two preferred. Mono, diethanolamine may cause skin irritation. Surfactants are used for improving properties such as emulsion stability. Humectants like glycerol, sorbitol, propylene glycol (3-10%) are used. Lubricants like lanolin, isopropyl myristate (1-2%) make passage of the razor over face easy. Propellants like fluorocarbons (7-10%), hydrocarbons (2.8-3.5%) are used in these formulations. Perfumes other agents like cooling agents (menthol), colours, preservatives may be used.

BATH PREPARATIONS

4.1 BATH OILS

Three types of bath oils may be distinguished: floating or spreading oil, dispersible, emulsifying or blooming oil and milky oil. The floating or spreading bath oils (usually mineral or vegetable oils or cosmetic esters such as isopropyl myristate) are the more effective for lubricating dry skin as well as carrying the fragrant. However, they suffer from "greasiness" and deposit formation around the bath tub. These problems are overcome by using self-emulsifying oils which are formulated with surfactant mixtures. When added to water they spontaneously emulsify forming small oil droplets that deposit on the skin surface. However, these self-emulsifying oils produce less emolliency compared with the floating oils. These bath oils usually contain a high level of fragrance since they are used in a large amount of water.

Bath oils can be classified into four main categories are as follows:

- Floating or spreading type bath oils
- Dispersible type bath oils
- Soluble type bath oils
- Foaming type bath

Ingredients	Per cent of Total
Isopropyl myristate	60.0
Oleyl alcohol	35.0
Perfume	5.0
Colour	q.s

Ingredients	Per cent of Total
Isopropyl myristate	35.0
Mineral oil	35.0
Diethyl phthalate	10.0
Perfume	20.0
Colour	q.s.

Ingredients	Per cent of Total
Triethanolamine oleate	10.0
Perfume oil	10.0
Water to make	100.0

Ingredients	Per cent of Total
Mineral oil	60.0
Isopropyl myristate	25.0
Brij 93	9.0
Perfume	6.0

4.2 BATH SOAPS

These are one of the oldest toiletries products that have been used over centuries, the earliest formulations were based on simple fatty acid salts, such as sodium or potasium palmitate. However, these simple soaps suffer from the problem of calcium soap precipitation in hard water. For that reason, most soap bars contain other surfactants such as cocomonoglyceride sulphate or sodium cocoglyreryl ether sulphonate that prevent precipitation with calcium ions. Other surfactants used in soap bars include sodium cocyl lsethinate, sodium dodecyl benzene sulphonate and sodium stearyl sulphate.

Several other functional ingredients are included in soap bar formulations, e.g. antibacterial, deodorants, lather enhancers, anti-irritancy materials, vitamins, etc. Other soap bar additives include antioxidants, chelating agents, opacifying agents (e.g. titanium dioxide), optical brighteners, binders, plasticizers etc.

4.3 BATH FOAM (OR BUBBLE)

These can be produced in the form of liquids, creams, gels, powders, granules (beads). Their main function is to produce maximum foam into running water. The basic surfactants used in bubble bath formulations are anionic, non-ionic or amphoteric together with some foam stabilizers, fragrant and suitable solubilizers. These formulations should be compatible with soap and they may contain other ingredients for enhancing skin care properties.

A good foam bath should have the following qualities:

- The bubble bath should form easily without requiring excessive water pressure.
- Foam should be stable irrespective of use hard or soft water and soap.
- The product should not form a ring around the bath tub.

- It should be non-irritating to the skin and mucous membrane in concentration used in bath tubs.

Liquid foam bath (bubble bath) is the most popular formulation.

Ingredients	Per cent of Total
Triethanolamine lauryl sulphate	55.0
Perfume	5.0
Water to make	40.0
Colour and preservatives	q.s.

Ingredients	Per cent of Total
Triethanolamine lauryl sulphate	35.0
Alkylolamide	3.0
Perfume	5.0
Water to make	100.0
Colour and preservatives	q.s.

4.4 AFTER BATH PREPARATIONS

These are formulations designed to counteract the damaging effects caused after bath, e.g. skin drying caused by removal of natural fats and oils from the skin. Several formulations may be used, e.g. lotions and creams, liquid splashes, dry oil spray, dusting powders or talc, etc. Lotions and creams, which are the most commonly used formulations are simply O/W emulsions with skin conditioners and emollients. The liquid splashes are hydro-alcoholic products that contain some oil to provide skin conditioning. They can be applied as a liquid spread on the skin by hand or by spraying.

CHAPTER **5**...

HAIR PRODUCTS

INTRODUCTION

Hair consists of tissues called epithelium, which corresponds to the cuticle of the epidermis. Hair has no blood vessels nor does nerve supply when hair is cut it continue to grow. Colour of hair is dependent on pigmentation. The composition of hair is probably uniform, when taken its cross section; it is divided into three sections known as cuticle, cortex and medulla. Hair consists of keratoid or protein and may be classified as coarse, medium and fine. Nourishment to hairs is gained by the capillaries of sebaceous gland surrounding hair bulb.

Hair Structure

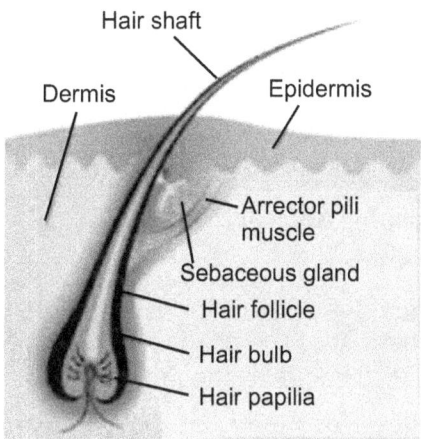

Fig. 5.1: Hair Structure

5.1 HAIR SHAMPOOS

Shampoos are most widely used cosmetic. Earlier soap cakes were used for washing hair, but now-a-days both men and women population mostly uses shampoos.

Functions

- It should remove soil and residues of hair setting lotions/dressing from hair and scalp.
- It should produce foam of degree that will satisfy the user.
- Shampoo should be easy to remove by rinsing, leaving the hair soft and manageable.
- It should impart pleasant fragrances during use masking the odour of wet hair.

The dirt basically consists of sebum secretion by the scalp, sweet residue, flakes of horny layers, residue from hair care cosmetics, dust and other external matter settled on hair and scalp.

Formulations of Shampoo

(a) Detergents/ Surfactants

Detergent involves the following properties:

(1) The detergent must wet both dirt as well as hair i.e. it should lower surface tension.

(2) The interfacial tension must be reduced, so that dirt or oil particles are displaced by detergent solution.

(3) The dirt particles must be kept dispersed so that these are washed away.

(4) The polar group of detergent has the ability to displace oil from the surface. These properties are important for hair washing.

Efficiency of detergents can be assess by performing the following tests:

➤ Ease of spreading

➤ Lathering power

➤ Efficient soil removal

➤ Ease of rinsing

➤ Ease of combing wet hairs

➤ Luster of the hairs

➤ Speed of drying

➤ Ease of combing and setting dry hairs

➤ Safety.

(i) Non-ionic: They have sufficient cleansing power but only a few have sufficient foaming properties. These are used as foam booster and stabilizers. These are mild and non-irritating. e.g. Fatty acid alkanolamides.

(ii) Cationics: They produces foam and have good cleansing power. They leave hair lustrous and free of electrostatic charge. Cationics are irritant in nature, particularly to corneal eye tissue. Non-ionics and cationics are used in combinations.

(iii) Anionic Surfactants: Due to superior foaming preparation and low cost anionics are most widely used :

• Alkyl benzene sulphonates

• Alkyl sulphate: Lauryl sulphate gives greater volume to lather and myristyl sulphate gives greater richness, so they are used in combination. Among all, SLS is better as flash foam and foam volume is concerned.

• Sulphosuccinates

• Acyl lactylates etc.

(iv) Amphoteric Surfactants: These are mild in nature and used in mild shampoo. e.g. n-alkyl amino acids, betains etc.

(b) Conditioning Agents

These agents are intended to improve manageability, feel and luster of the hair. e.g. Lanolin, mineral oil etc.

(c) Viscosity Modifiers

Different viscosity modifiers are Electrolytes – NH_4Cl, $NaCl$; Natural gums e.g. karaya, tragacanth, alginates etc.; Cellulose derivatives like HEC, HPC, CMC etc.; Carboxyvinyl polymers etc.

(d) Opacifying and Clarifying Agents

These agents gives pearlescent effect. Opacifying agents are fatty alcohol (cetyl, stearyl); veegum, alkanolamides of higher fatty acids etc., and clarifying agent are ethanol, IPA, Propylene glycol, hexylene glycols etc.

(e) Sequestering Agents

These materials are used to prevent deposition of calcium and magnesium salts of soaps on the hair e.g. EDTA, polyphosphates etc.

(f) Preservatives

As surfactants in shampoo tend to interfere with bacterial activity, higher concentration of preservatives is necessary. e.g. Formaldehyde (0.1 – 0.15%), Parabens but these are inactivated by non-ionics.

(g) Perfumes

Fragrance used should be soluble in shampoo and compatible also. It should not affect viscosity and stability. e.g. Herbal, Floral fragrance (0.3 – 1.0%).

Formulations

(a) Powder Shampoo

These are dry shampoo. These should be removed by brushing. These contain adsorbent materials like starch, talc, keiselguhr etc.

Ingredients	Per cent of Total
Sodium bicarbonate	45
Disodium phosphate	20
Soap powder	35
Perfumes	q.s.

Ingredients	Per cent of Total
SLS	20
Sarcoside	5
Sodium bicarbonate	10
Sodium sulphate	65
Perfumes	q.s.

Mix all ingredients together and add perfume finally.

(b) Clear Liquid Shampoo

These are prepared with detergents having lower cloud point. Concentrated clear liquid shampoo can be prepared with more soluble monoethanolanine lauryl sulphate. pH of shampoo preparation plays an important role. Shampoo having higher pH tend to damage hair and skin. Mild acidity prevents swelling and penetration. Low pH is favourable and imparts conditioning effects.

Ingredients	Per cent of Total
Triethanolamine lauryl sulphate	45
Coconut monoethanolamide	2
Water to make	100
Perfumes, colours and preservatives	q.s.

Ingredients	Per cent of Total
Sodium lauryl ether sulphate	40
Sodium chloride	2.0-4.0
Water to make	100
Perfumes, colours and preservatives	q.s.

Ingredients	Per cent of Total
Monoethanolamine lauryl sulphate	70
Coconut monoethanolamide	2
Water to make	100
Perfumes, colours and preservatives	q.s.

(c) Liquid Cream or Lotion Shampoo

These are prepared by adding opacifier to clear liquid shampoo. Ethylene glycol monostearates, ethylene glycol distearates used as opacifiers. These opacifiers have tendency to redissolve in hot weather so magnesium stearate should be added.

Ingredients	Per cent of Total
Monoethanolamine lauryl sulphate	45
Ethylene glycol monostearate	5
Water to make	100
Perfumes, colours and preservatives	q.s.

Ingredients	Per cent of Total
Monoethanolamine lauryl sulphate	35
Glyceryl monostearate	2
Magnesium stearates	1
Water to make	100
Perfumes, colours and preservatives	q.s.

Mucilaginous thickeners can be used like PVA, MC, alginates, magnesium stearates etc. Opacifying effects of higher alcohol or alcohol esters can be improved with lanolin, glycol/glyceryl laurate (1-2%). Shampoo can also contain other additives like egg, milk, cream, coconut etc.

(d) Cream Shampoo / Shampoo paste

Sodium alkyl sulphates are used which gives firm consistency. Cetyl alcohol added as a builder. Foam stabilizers used are coconut diethanolamide and lauric isopropanolamide (1-2%).

Ingredients	Per cent of Total
SLS	38
Cetyl alcohol	7
Water to make	100
Colour, Perfumes and Preservatives	q.s.

(e) Jelly Shampoo

Thickening agents like hydroxyl-alkyl or methyl cellulose ethers or combination of anionic and amphoteric surfactants can also produce gels.

Ingredients	Per cent of Total
Alkyl dimethyl Benzalkonium chloride	15
Triethanolamine lauryl sulphate (40%)	28
Coconut diethanolamide	7
HPMC	1
Water to make	100
Colour, perfumes and preservatives	q.s.

Anti-dandruff Shampoo

If the process of keratinization and shedding off of hairs increases to an abnormal rate, cells become visible in the form of flaky scales. Such conditions cause dandruff. In another condition, abnormal secretion of sebum from sebaceous gland called as seborrhoea. The abnormal conditions of scalp are associated with an increase in the growth of bacteria and fungi. This may lead to acne and psoriasis.

A medicated shampoo is regard to have the following functions:

(1) It should clean both, the hair and the scalp and should leave hair manageable.

(2) It should not irritate sebaceous gland.

(3) It should contain an anti-microbial to prevent growth of increased incidence of microbes.

(4) Active ingredients should be non-sensitizing and non-irritating.

Materials used in the Treatment of Dandruff are

- ➢ Thymol   0.05 – 0.2%
- ➢ Pyrithione zinc   2.0%
- ➢ Resorcinol   0.05 – 1.0%
- ➢ Selenium sulphide   1.0 – 2.5%
- ➢ Quaternary Ammonium compounds   15 – 20%

Camphor as counter irritant and menthol as cooling agent can be used. Cationic surfactants possess varying degree of bactericidal action. Quaternary ammonium compounds are non-irritant and non-toxic. e.g. cetrimide, benzalkonium chloride, stearyl dimethyl benzyl amino chloride etc.

Ingredients	Per cent of Total
Thymol	0.1
Camphor	0.1
Triethanolamine lauryl sulphate	60
Water to make	100
Colours, perfumes and preservatives	q.s.

Ingredients	Percent of Total
Thymol	0.05
Camphor	0.1
Menthol	0.1
Triethanolamine lauryl sulphate	55
Water to make	100
Colours, perfumes and preservatives	q.s.

Thymol, menthol and camphor can be dissolved in alcohol / mixed with perfume and added to remaining ingredients.

Conditioning Shampoos

These primarily cleanse and secondarily improve manageability, feel and appearance of hair. Quaternary ammonium compounds are conditioner and bactericidal. Quaternary ammonium compounds are absorbed onto the hair fibres, removes static charge thereby reduces friction between hair strands. Thus, leaves hairs more manageable.

Ingredients	Per cent of Total
Stearyl dimethly benzyl ammonium chloride	5.5
Ethylene glycol monostearate	2.0
Cetyl alcohol	2.5
Water to make	100
Preservatives and Perfumes	q.s.

Hair Colourants

In general, hair colourants are used for the following purposes:

(1) Change the natural colour of hair.

(2) Colour grey colour.

(3) To change colour of hair for a particular occasion.

Ideal Characteristics

(1) It should colour the hair without reducing natural glass and without impairing its texture.

(2) It should not injure the hair shaft.

(3) It should be non-irritant and free from sensitizing action.

(4) It should not have systemic toxicity.

(5) Colour of the dyed hair should be stable to physical factors like air, sunlight, friction and chemical factors like sweat.

(6) It should not change colour on application of shampoos setting, lotions etc.

(1) Temporary Hair Colorants (THC)

Temporary colours do not penetrate in the cortex / medulla, they are absorbed onto or become substantive to hair cuticle, because of these, they can removed easily with a shampoo, hence known as THC.

The dye stuff used includes basic dyes, acidic dyes, disperse dyes, metallized (pigments) and belong largely to azo, anthraquinones, biphenyl methane dyes etc. These are formulated in different forms like powders, crayons, liquids and shampoos.

Crayons

Ingredients	Per cent of Total
Stearic acid	15
Triethanolamine	7
Bees wax	50
Carnauba wax	13
Ozokerite	7
Glyceryl monostearate	6
Gum tragacanth	2
Colour	q.s.

Liquid Rinses

Ingredient	Per cent of Total
Dye stuff (acidic)	6
Acetic acid	10
Ethyl alcohol	10
Water to make	100

(2) Semi-Permanent Hair Colorants

These products are designed to give stronger, more permanent colouration to hair than colour shampoo. Some colour will be removed in each shampooing and will be removed completely in 6-8 hours shampooing. Dyes which are used nitrophenylenediamines, nitroaminophenols aminoanthraquinone classes.

Factors to be considered before using any dyes,

- Solubility of dyes in water
- Compatibilities
- Composition of vehicle or base
- Effect of pH value on dye
- Effect of solvents which may be added to the formulation.

Ingredient	Per cent of Total
Quaternary amino compound	10-12
Anionic surfactants	8-10
Acid	6-8
Alkanolamide	4-6
Dye stuff	1-2
Water to make	100

(3) Permanent Hair Colorants

In olden days permanent hair dyes were obtained from plants e.g. Henna leaves. Henna is non-toxic and does not cause sensitization reaction. Repeated use of Henna packs may give an un-natural reddish brown colour and may cause staining of hands, fingers and nails.

Light Brown Colour		Dark Brown		Black	
Powered Henna	90.0 gm	Powered Henna	83.0 gm	Powered Henna	73.0 gm
Pyrogallol	5.0 gm	Pyrogallol	10.0 gm	Pyrogallol	15.0 gm
Copper sulphate	5.0 gm	Copper sulphate	7.0 gm	Copper sulphate	12.0 gm

Evaluation

(a) Skin irritation test

Draize test in rabbits (patch test techniques)

A set of three rabbits used for testing each material

Shampoos should be tested for short duration

The product should be in contact for not more than four hours

Preparations are diluted before use

The patch is removed after four hours and score are given on skin condition (oedema, erythema or eschac formation).

The product may be classified as mild irritant, moderate irritant and severe irritant.

(b) Skin sensitization test: Skin sensitivity should be checked.

(c) Eye irritating test: Draize test in rabbits

5.2 HAIR TONIC

Most of hair tonics are hydro alcoholic solution and can be manufactured in stainless steel mixing vessel with a stirrer. As alcoholic preparations are easily flammable, these are to be used with precaution.

Following are few specifications which are to be applied and considered during the manufacturing of hair tonics.

➢ Whenever there is use of fats and oils, optimum temperature should be maintained.

➢ Viscosity, stability and shelf like are greatly affected by rate and manner of agitation used.

➢ When dispersion is important, colloid mill should be used because smaller the particle size, better the dispersion.

5.3 HAIR DYES

Commonly hair dyes are either in liquid form or in powder form. There are two types of liquid hair dyes:

(1) Type-1 (black)

(2) Type-2 (brown)

In these dyes, the active ingredient usually is an aryl amine dispersed in suitable surface active in an alkaline medium. Type-2 dyes may contain dye chemicals like, ortho-amino phenol, p-amino phenol etc. They contain suitable modifiers like resorcinol. Usually, developers packed these two ingredients separately and these are supposed to be mixed in water before use.

Indian standard for powder hair dye is 10350-1993. The pH range of 5% solution in water is 7 to 10 for type 1 to type 2.

The main requirements of powder dyes:

(a) Fine,

(b) Free flowing

(c) Colouring property.

Caution

While using hair dye some caution to be carried.

Before using dye product, skin irritation and skin sensitizing test is to be carried out. Small sample applied on small patch of hair on scalp and after application skin irritation is observed if any.

5.4 DEPILATORIES

Preparations for the removal of unwanted hair have been known for thousands of years. Among them was rhusma a mixture of quick time and arsenical pyrites in a ratio of 1 : 2 used in ancient times by the dancing girls of the east (before use reduced to powder, mixed with an aqueous alkali, possibly obtained from wood ashes). Another preparation was orpiment (Arsenic Trisulphide).

Epilation

The process, in which the hair is removed by uprooting, is called **epilation** and the products used for epilation called **epilatories**.

Epilation has some drawbacks because the effect may be slight longer lasting since, if the epilated hair take with the hair bulb or the hair papillae, there may be a relatively long pause before the hair starts growing in follicle and reaches the surface of the skin. It is however painful and can often cause serious skin damage and subsequent infection. Epilatories are adhesive compositions to which the hairs stick when these are applied to them, then so stuck hairs are pulled mechanically.

Formulation

For many years epilators have been prepared with rosin and waxes. Mineral or vegetable oils can be incorporated in formulations.

Formula 1

Ingredients	Percent of Total
Rosin	50
Bees wax (yellow)	25
Paraffin wax	20
Petroleum jelly	5
Perfume	q.s

Formula 2

Ingredients	Per cent of Total
Rosin	62
Bees wax	10
Linseed oil	25
Camphor	1
Benzocaine	2

Camphor is used to give cooling effect as well as to reduce discomfort when the hair is pulled. Benzocaine used as a local anesthetic (to further reduce pain). Addition of an antibacterial will prevent infection of the damaged skin.

How to apply/Use?

When required, these waxes are first softened by heating and are spread evenly over the selected area with a suitable brush. When the applied mixture is cooled it is removed quickly. There has been no dramatic development in this type of formulations. However, there have been developments regarding modification in the method of application (flexible backing strip which can be applied and removed easily). Preparation being based upon a mixture of glucose and zinc oxide does not require melting prior to use.

Manufacture

Resin Wax Based Epilatories

Melting of resin and high melting point waxes in jacketed vessels.

⇩

Addition of ingredients like petroleum jelly, oil with stirring

If formulation contains camphor, benzocaine, these are dissolved in a part of oil and are added when temperature drops to around 45°C. Stirring is continued and the product is filled into jars.

Electrolysis

Mechanical methods are temporary and often only relatively effective since the papillae and hair bulbs are not always removed and hairs reappear. Most effective method of depilation is Electrolysis. Mechanism is insertion of needle into the hair follicle and complete destruction of the hair root by means of a weak DC current.

This method is practiced in beauty salons by some dermatologist. It is expensive and time consuming. Also, skill operator is required.

Depilatories

The process in which the hair (superfluous hair i.e the hair occurring on the face and legs as well as in axilla) are removed by chemical degradation without causing injury to the skin is called depilation and depilatory.

The term depilatory must therefore be reserved for chemical means of hair removal from skin (in particular superfluous hair occurring on the face, legs, axilla, etc.), without causing any injury to the skin. It is definitely different from other methods of hair removal, which includes,

- Mechanical removal of hair
- Destruction of hair by use of laser energy
- Shaving

Mechanism of Action

Hair is composed primarily of proteins (88%). These proteins are of a hard fibrous type known as keratin. Keratin proteins form cytoskeleton of all epidermal cells. The amino acid, cysteine is a key component of the keratin proteins in hair fibre. The sulfur in the cysteine molecule links together by disulfide chemical bonds. These disulfide bonds are very strong and very difficult to break apart. These disulfide chemical bonds linking the keratins together are the key factor in the durability and resistance of hair fibre to degradation under environmental stress. They are largely resistant to the action of acids but the disulfide bonds can be broken apart by alkali solutions. Hence, care should be taken, while formulating a depilatory, to ensure that the preparation reacts with the hair preferentially and that its effects will be sufficiently rapid to cause disintegration of the hair, before causing any damage to the underlying and the surrounding skin.

Chemical Depilation

The term depilatory refers to preparations intended for the chemical breakdown of superfluous hair without injury to skin.

Advantages

They avoid any danger of cutting or abrading the skin in regions such as underarms, where it is difficult to see the area clearly and even more difficult to guide a raiser over the complicated counters. It is belief that shaving increases the rate of hair growth or the coarseness of the hair. Chemical depilatories discourage the regrowth of hair if they are applied regularly.

Disadvantages

Since, the hair shaft is of similar composition to the skin, a small degree of local damage may occur as a result of applying such a preparation. Particularly, if the depilatory is kept in contact with the skin for any length of time and the pH is sufficiently high, then horny layer of skin also be attacked. Provided that the skin is reasonably healthy, that the time of application of the depilatory is not too long and this is correctly formulated.

Ideal Requirements of a Depilatory

- Non-toxic and non-irritant to skin
- Efficient, removing hair rapidly, preferably in 4 to 6 minutes.
- Preferably odourless
- Stable on storage
- Harmless to clothing
- Cosmetically elegant.

Formulation

The alkaline reducing agent cause hair fibres to swell to produce a cleavage of the cystine bridges between adjacent polypeptide chains leads to the complete degradation of the hair. The common agents are given as follows:

(I) Alkaline Reducing Agent

(a) Sulphides

- Sulphides of metals like sodium, potassium, magnesium, calcium, strontium, barium, aluminium, arsenic produce depilation which is accelerated in the presence of $Ca(OH)_2$ suspension.
- The alkali sulphides such as sodium sulphide where found to be drastic in action. Their depilatory action is link to the hydrolysis and the formation of sulphydrates and NaOH. Although, it will disintegrate hair within 6-7 minutes it will simultaneously damage the stratum corneum. It is therefore no longer used.
- Strontium sulphide (3-5 min.) is much milder depilatory must be used at a higher concentration than Na_2S to produce an equivalent dehairing action. Strontium hydroxide crystalline in the preparations made with strontium sulphide. Milling may

control this problem at the time of manufacture but crystals reappear on storage with temperature fluctuations.

- Use of barium sulphide has been discontinued as it is poisonous.

The main reason for the loss in popularity of sulphide based depilatories is that they generate odour of H_2S on application. This odour is most intense when the product is washed off, owing to hydrolysis of sulphide.

Remedy

Remove the bulk of the product with a spatula before washing and it is usual practice to include such a spatula made of wood or plastic in the pack. It also serves to apply the product in the necessary thick layer. Despite their disadvantage, sulphide based depilatories are preferred by many black-skinned men for removing facial hair because of their comparatively rapid action.

(b) Stannites

Since, stannates have no appreciable odour, attempts are made to overcome the disadvantage of sulphide which have strong foul odour by using sodium stannites.

(c) Substituted Mercaptans

The majority of depilatories available today are substituted mercaptans which acts in alkaline pH. Mercaptans have less odour but take more time for depilation. The preparations based on mercaptons are safer than sulphides on the skin and therefore can be used on even face where women have an aversion for using razer.

(d) Thioglycolates

Thioglycolate based preparations are non-toxic and stable at concentrations at which they are used, that is between 2.5 and 4 per cent.

At concentrations of less than 2%w/w, they act too slowly to be of any use, while nothing will be gained in terms of effectiveness their concentration is raised above 4%. At this concentration, these preparations produce depilation between 5-15 minutes depending upon pH of preparation. Higher the pH, faster the depilation. The pH should not be less than 10. It should be around 12.5.

(II) Perfumes

Most of the alkaline reducing agents, including salts of thioglycolic acid, have usually an odour of their own, while many others, particularly sulphides, generate the odour of hydrogen sulphide on application. Hence, the use of perfumes is almost a necessity in depilatory products. The perfume materials used are aromatic alcohols, ketones, anise, safrol and rose. With improved manufacturing technology, the cosmetic industry has arrived at products (such as calcium thioglycolate) which are far less malodorous than what was previously available.

(III) Emulsifiers

The common emulsifiers used are mainly ethylene oxide ethers of fatty alcohol soaps, sodium lauryl sulphate and other anionics are rarely used for reasons of cosmetic elegancy and potential irritancy.

(IV) Emollients

The common emollients used are mineral oils and paraffins.

(V) Thickening agents

Synthetic thickening agents, such as methyl, hydroxyl ethyl or carboxyl methyl cellulose are used. The earlier formulations employed the use of materials such as zinc stearates, talc, colloidal clay, titanium dioxide, starch, precipitated chalk, etc., or a suitable combination of these to make a paste of requisite consistency.

(VI) Humectants

Humectants such as glycerin, sorbitol, propylene glycol, etc., are incorporated to prevent quick drying on the skin.

Miscellaneous

Some other common ingredients of a depilatory product includes:

➤ Enzymes

➤ Accelerators

➤ Hair growth retardants.

The depilatory agent must conform to certain general rules are as follows:

- pH value should be between 9-12.5.
- Concentration of mercaptans should be between 0.1 and 1.5 mol/litre.
- The alkaline ingredient must have an ionization constant greater than 2×10^{-5}.
- Paste form is most satisfactory.
- Natural gums are used to give stable formulations.
- In order to prevent skin damage, is desirable that the concentration of alkaline material in solution be not greater than twice the equivalent concentration of the mercaptans.

Depilatory Powder

Ingredients	Per cent of Total
Titanium dioxide	23
Barium sulfide	35
Wheat starch	40
Menthol	0.2
Perfume	1.8

Method

Dissolve the menthol in perfume oil and add some starch to it by rubbing. Sift the titanium dioxide and barium sulfide together. Then mix and sift the remaining starch, and next add it to the menthol-perfume mixture. Mix the entire batch for about half an hour, and then pack.

Depilatory Paste

Ingredients	Per cent of Total
Strontium sulphide	20
Talc	20
Methyl cellulose	3
Glycerine	15
Water	42

Method

Dissolve methyl cellulose into water and mix glycerin. Sift strontium sulphide and talc into the above mixture slowly and stir thoroughly, until a smooth paste is obtained.

Depilatory Lotion

	Ingredients	Per cent of Total
A	Magnesium aluminum silicate	1
	Deionized water	74
B	Propylene glycol	5
C	Mineral oil and lanolin alcohol	5
	Polysorbate 80 and Cetyl acetate	2
	Glyceryl stearates and PEG 100 stearate	2
D	Calcium thioglycolate	5
	Calcium hydroxide	6
E	Preservative, dye and Fragrance to make	100

Method

Slowly add magnesium aluminum silicate to the water, while agitating at maximum available shear. Continue mixing until smooth. Add (B) to (A). Heat (C) to 70°C, then add with stirring. Cool to 45°C add calcium thioglycolate and stir. Add calcium hydroxide, stir until cool and uniform, add (E).

Typical Formula Based on Thioglycolate

Ingredients	Per cent of Total
Calcium thioglycolate	15
Calcium hydroxide	22
Strontium hydroxide	10
SLS	1.5
Hydroxy methyl cellulose	1
Magnesium carbonate	51
Perfume	q.s.

Method

Mix thioglycolate, hydroxides, SLS and hydroxyl methyl cellulose in a binder. Blend perfume separately with Mg carbonate add this to former mix and blend thoroughly. It is difficult to perfume depilatories satisfactorily. Strong floral type perfumes like rose, violet type excluding ingredient which are prone to hydrolysis themselves are suitable for the sulphide based depilatories. Perfume used should be stable at high pH and should have strong odour. The formula is required to buffer between pH 7-8.

Packaging

Lotion depilatories are generally packed in jars and creams are packed in collapsible tubes. When creams are prepared without addition of antioxidant, air slowly gets access into the jars through caps and creams turn yellow, first at the surface then slowly inside. Remedy is addition of steric hydroxide. Depilatories should be filled promptly after homogenization. Tin or plastic can be used. Packing in laminated tube is more common.

Evaluation

1. Prophetic
2. Diagnostic

Depilatories containing sulphides of alkali, thioglycolate are capable for acting as primary irritants. Closed patch test for diagnostic purpose is not recommended.

1. For testing new depilatories actual user test should be carried out with well establish depilatory in market as control.
2. Before actual user test, carry out prophetic patch test on 10 subjects to evaluate irritant properties of new depilatory by using proper control. (i.e marketed preparation).

Profetic Patch Test

1. Prepare inactive base of depilatory. Prepare dilutions of control as follows:

    One part depilatory + one part base, one part depilatory + two parts base

    One part depilatory + three parts base ………… One part depilatory + n parts of base

2. Place patches of well established depilatory dilutions on one thigh and patches of test depilatory on another thigh of the subject. Examine the patches after 24-48 hours.

3. Finished depilatories are tested for pH by pH meter. pH should not exceed 12.7.

4. Contents of depilating agent should be determined by chemical analysis.

CHAPTER **6...**

EYE PRODUCTS

INTRODUCTION

Eye makeup is an essential item of facial makeup. Most commonly used eye cosmetics are,

1. Eye brow pencil
2. Eye shadow
3. Eye liner
4. Eye mascara

Eye is very sensitive organ. Therefore, cosmetics for eye should be made from pure, safe, non-toxic and non-irritating materials. Before use of materials, these should be tested for their harmlessness.

Following ingredients are commonly used in eye cosmetics:

1. **Fats and Waxes**: They are used to contribute the structure of eye cosmetics.
   - **Petrolatum (M.P. 43°C).**
   - **Lanolin (M.P. 38-40°C):** Used in eye shadow and mascara for lubricating and adhering qualities.
   - **Ceresin (M.P. 68°C):** Stiffen the preparation without making too brittle/ hard.
   - **Carnauba wax (M.P. 85°C):** Forms water repellent film, gives luster to the dried application.
   - **Bees wax (M.P. 64°C):** Stiffens the preparation without hardening. Used in product to be molded (cake mascara).
   - **Stearic acid (M.P. 55°C):** Saponify easily, gives stable soap.
     Example: Triethanolamine stearate.

2. **Liquid components:** They acts as solvent or dispersing agent for insoluble pigments.
   Examples: Castor oil, mineral oil, isopropyl myristate etc.

3. **Softening agents:** These are higher fatty acid and fatty materials which included in eye cosmetics to make it softer and spread easily leaving the gloss on surface. Examples: Petroleum, lanolin etc.

4. **Gums** These are two types 1) Natural, 2) Synthetic. Examples: Tragacanth, methyl cellulose etc.

5. **Pigment:** The main purpose of pigment is to give intensity and variation of colour. Titanium oxide and zinc oxide are used to get lighter shades.
   - Black: carbon black, charcoal black, iron oxide black.

> ➤ Blue: ultramarine blue.
> ➤ Green: chromium oxide.
> ➤ Brown: iron oxide.
> ➤ Yellow: iron oxide.
> ➤ Red: carmine.

Fig. 6.1

6. **Preservatives:** Not used in all eye cosmetics. i.e. Methyl/ Propyl parabens
7. **Perfumes:** It may cause irritation so it should be selected with care.

6.1 EYE MASCARA

It is black pigmented preparation. It is applied on eye lashes. It darkens eye lashes and gives an illusion of their greater density and length. "Mascara is used to accentuate eyelashes and make them more visible; more pronounced thereby enhancing the character of eyes".

Fig. 6.2

Characteristics

- Easy to apply and capable of even application possible.
- Dry quickly and should not cake.
- Non-toxic and non-irritant.
- It should not cause smudging.

Types of Mascara

- Cake
- Cream
- Liquid.

(i) Cake Mascara

Early mascaras were cake composed of soap and pigments. Soap have higher pH (around 10) therefore such product cause irritation. Tears, rains, etc could cause smudging. Cake mascara is to be applied with wet brush.

Ingredients	Per cent of Total
Carbon black	55
Coconut oil sodium soap	22.5
Palm oil sodium soap	22.5

Coconut oil sodium soap and Palm oil sodium soap are replaced with triethanolamine stearates which are less alkaline.

Ingredients	Per cent of Total
Triethanolamine stearate	55
Carnauba wax	24.5
Paraffin wax	12.5
Lanolin anhydrous	4.5
Carbon black	3.5
Preservatives	q.s.

Manufacturing of Cake Mascara

Waxes are melted.

↓

Pigments are dispersed in it by means of roller mill.

↓

The grounded material is remelted and poured into mould with slow stirring.

↓

It is applied with wet brush.

(ii) Cream Mascara

Mix the pigment into cream base. It may contain oil soluble dyes. It is necessary to include wetting agent to lower the surface tension. Lotion type cream can be prepared by adding film forming agent, e.g. PVP. Waterproof mascara can be prepared with anhydrous base and silica fluid with given water repellency.

Ingredients	Per cent of Total
Stearic acid	12
Isopropyl myristate	6
Glyceryl monostearate	5.5
Glycerin	5.5
Trimethanolamine	3.5
Water	57.5
Pigments	10
Preservatives	q.s.

A lotion type cream with good lasting properties can be prepared by adding poly vinyl alcohol or polyvinyl acetate to an emulsion based on TEA.

Ingredients	Per cent of Total
Stearic acid	3
Isopropyl myristate	3.5
TEA	1
polyvinyl acetate	5.5
Water to make	100
Pigments	10
Perfumes and preservatives	q.s.

(iii) Liquid Mascara

It is prepared by suspending pigment in mucilage so sticky preparation is formed.

Ingredients	Per cent of Total
Gum tragacanth	0.3
Alcohol	10
Lamp/Carbon black	8
Water to make	100
Preservatives	q.s.

These preparations are aqueous and tends to smudge so alcoholic solution of resins can be used.

Method: Resin is dissolved in alcohol with stirring. Lamp black poured into castor oil with continuous stirring till it mixed well.

Ingredients	Per cent of Total
Rosin (10% solution in alcohol)	3.5
Castor oil	2.5
Lamp /Carbon black	12
Alcohol	82

Drawback: May irritate eye if accidently dropped in eye.

Evaluation

Flexibility and adhesion: A useful test for flexibility and adhesion is to coat the mascara on a clean keratin surface and to allow it to dry. The mascara film is then viewed under stereomicroscope and using pointed object, a circle of approximately 6 mm is drawn on the mascara film, penetrating to the surface of the keratin. The disc of mascara is reduced in size, using the needle until small disc of mascara flakes off the keratin surface. The size of this final disc provides surprisingly good indicator of how well product adheres. The remorbility of the mascara with water, oil, emulsion based cleanser can also be checked on lashes.

Viscosity and consistency: While high viscosity will cause the lashes to stick together. The viscosity should be choosen such that it gives good definitions and coverage but will not cause the lashes to stick together. The effect of the products viscosity on ease of application and transfer from brush to lashes should be checked. If the texture is very short, efficient transfer will be difficult; conversely if the texture is long and stringy, the lashes will tend to stick together. If mascara mass leaves small peaks when fingers are placed on the surface and withdrawn, then application characteristics will usually be satisfactory.

6.2 EYE SHADOW

"Eye shadow is cosmetic which is applied on the upper eyelid and under the eyebrows or around the eyes to look eyes more attractive". It is used to give background of colour to the eye. It adds colour and personality to the face. It is available in various colours such as blue, green, brown etc.

Fig. 6.3

Types of Eye Shadow

- Solid: Powder compact, stick or pencil.
- Liquid: Oil based or emulsion type o/w or w/o.

Ideal Characteristics

- It should have good skin adhesion and easy to apply.
- It should not oily after application.
- Non-irritant and safe.
- It should not smudge by sweat and should maintain good appearance.

Formulations

(a) Cream eye shadow

(b) Stick eye shadow

(c) Liquid eye shadow

(d) Powder eye shadow

(a) Cream Eye Shadow

It is liquefying cream or emulsion. It includes waxes and fatty materials.

(i) Liquefying cream bases are as given. To these bases pigments are added.

Ingredients	Per cent of Total
Petrolatum	47
Lanolin liquid	4.5
Bees wax	4.5
Microcrystalline wax	8.5
IPM	35

Ingredients	Per cent of Total
Lanolin anhydrous	10
Spermaceti wax	13
Petrolatum	77

Manufacturing of Cream Eye Shadow

Pigment are mixed and blended with petroleum in roller mill.

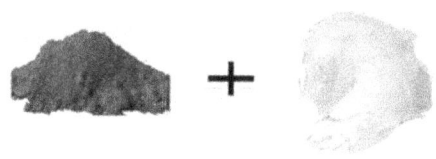 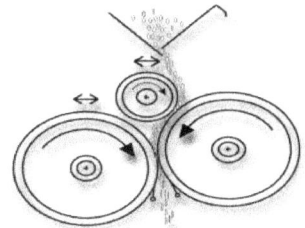

Fig. 6.4

↓

Other fatty materials are melted in pan and are blended

↓

The pigments mass is transferred to the molten fats and stirred well

↓

Fill into the container while hot (Emulsion cream eye shadow should be filled cold in container).

(ii) Emulsion type of eye shadow creams can be prepared by mixing pigments into an emulsion and distributing them into the base

Ingredients	Per cent of Total
Stearic acid	2.5
Mineral oil	9.5
Lanolin	1.5
Glyceryl monostearate	3.0
Glycerin	5.0
Triethanolamine	0.5
Water to make	100
Perfumes and preservatives	q.s.

10 parts of pigments can be mixed with 100 parts of above base.

Different pigments and shades are:

Ultramarine (20 parts) + titanium dioxide = Blue

Titanium dioxide (15 parts) + chromium oxide (10 parts) = Green

(b) Stick Eye Shadow

It contains wax or fatty materials for ease of application. Base should be thixotropic so that it is applied without being greasy or sticky.

Fig. 6.5

Ingredients	Per cent of Total
Castor oil	42
Mineral oil	6
Hydrogenated cotton seed oil	6
Ceresin	25
Carnauba wax	5
TiO_2	9
Iron oxide (Ochre shade)	4
Iron oxide (Sienna shade)	3
Preservatives and antioxidants	q.s.

Manufacturing of Stick Eye Shadow

Melt ceresin and carnauba wax

↓

Prepare paste of pigments using oil components

↓

Add into above molten wax and grind using roller mill

↓

Remelt and pour into the mold

(c) Liquid Eye Shadow

It contains pigment dispersed in mixture of oil or in liquid emulsion. In such products, pigments are generally settled. So label must carry instructions, "Shake well before use".

Ingredients	Per cent of Total
Mineral oil	60
Corn oil	18
Isopropyl myristate	22
Pigments	q.s.
Preservatives	q.s.

Manufacturing of Liquid Eye Shadow

Grind pigments and add into part of oil to form pourable paste

↓

Add this to oil mixture

↓

Filled into container

(d) Powder Eye Shadow

- Loose powder
- Compressed powder.

Fig. 6.6

Ingredients	Per cent of Total
Kaolin	16
Zinc stearate	7
Talc	32
Pigment	12
Luster pigment	28
Pearlescent pigment	5

Above formula can be converted into compressed powder using **binding agents** such as Lanolin esters or base composed of bees wax, lanolin and mineral oil. It also blends on to the eyebrow. In this, veegum (Mg Al silicate) acts on binder giving a full cake with good pay off.

Ingredients	Per cent of Total
Veegum	7
Kaolin	10
Zinc stearates	10
Zinc oxide	5
Talc	50
Pigment	18
Preservative	q.s.

Evaluation

Colour testing: Products are placed on white paper and pressed flat with palette knife. Shades are compared to one another. Shades and blushers are checked on the skin.

Bulk density: It is carried out loose powder to ensure that no entrapped air is present so that incorrect filling weights are minimized.

Penetration and Drop test: It is carried out in pressed powder. Penetrometer is used to determine the accuracy of pressure during filling. Drop test is used to determine physical strength of cake.

6.3 EYE LINER

They are used on the top lid of each eye and sometimes under the lower lashes. The line should be smooth. These are used to make the eye prominent and create on illusion on thicker lashes.

Ideal Characteristics

- Non-irritant.
- Dry quickly, easy to apply.
- Films should have flexibility.
- It should last well, not peel off, smudge or crack.
- There should be no separation of pigments.
- Less microbial contamination as possible.

Fig. 6.7

Types of Eye Liner

1. Solid: a) Powder compact
           b) Pencil type.
2. Liquid: a) Oil based
           b) Water based
               (i) Film type
               (ii) Non-film type.

Formulation

   (i)   Liquid eye liner

  (ii) Cake eye liner

 (iii) Softer wax based eye pencil

 (iv) Khol eye liner.

(i) Liquid Eye Liner

It is available in liquid form. It gives the most intense and precise line that preferably defines the eye and stay sharp overtime. It also gives harsh line. It is difficult to apply and require steady.

Ingredients	Per cent of Total
Polyvinyl pyrolidone (PVP)	2
Magnesium aluminium silicate	2
Glycerin	4.5
Lanolin	0.5
Diethylene glycol monostearate	3
SLS	1
Pigment	12
Water to make	100
Preservatives	q.s.

Manufacturing of Liquid Eye Liner

Disperse Mg aluminium silicate in part of water to produce suspension

↓

Dissolve PVP in it and heat gently

↓

Add above mixture to molten stearate and lanolin

↓

Dissolve preservatives in glycerin and disperse pigments,
add dispersed pigments to above mixture

↓

Finally, dissolve SLS in small quantity of water and mix.

Ingredients	Per cent of Total
Polyvinyl pyrolidone (PVP)	2
Magnesium aluminium silicate	2.5
Glycerin	2.5
Lanolin	0.5
Diethylene glycol monostearates	3
Colloidal Silica	0.5
SLS	1
Pigment	14
Magnesium Carbonate	2.5
Water to make	100
Preservatives	q.s.

Pigments are disperse with colloidal silica and light magnesium carbonate rest procedure is same as above.

(ii) Cake Eye Liner

It is available in cake form. It contains high proportion of pigments and solution of binding agents. It is hard in nature. It is prepared by blending the pigment, other powered material. These are applied with wet brush.

Ingredients	Per cent of Total
Kaolin	5
Zinc stearate	12
Precipitated calcium carbonate	7
Pigments	10
Talc to make	100

(iii) Soft Wax Based Eye Pencil

It contains wax, that ease of application.

(iv) Kohl Eye Liner

It has softest powder texture. It is available in several form pencil, pressed or loosed powder. It is usually applied to the inner rim of the eye (pink area behind the eye lashes)

Evaluation

Hardness and Consistency

Hardness and consistency should be checked for test sample before their insertion into the pencil casing. Pencil cut in half, to inspect for undispersed pigments particles. If pencil formulation will sharpen easily, time after time, indicates it is good formulation.

Drop test is also carried out for testing break strength. The degree of drop is measured and determined visually and grade is assigned. Out of specification drop can indicate leads that will give poor colour pay off.

Pencils should be maintained and monitored at the elevated temperature, such as 37-50°C, for evaluating shrinking, melting, oil separation and pigments bleeding.

6.4 EYEBROW PENCIL

They are used for colouring the eyebrows and eyelids. "Eyebrow pencils are used to accentuate the natural eyebrow line or to modify it after plucking". Available either in crayon type or ordinary pencil type. Manufactured in many shades black to brownish black and brown to blue.

Functions

- Emphasize eyebrows.
- Improve their shape.
- Makes them look thick.

Fig. 6.8

The colour of eyebrow pencil should never be darker than that of your eyebrows. The popularity of pencil depending on their hardness and colour composition.

Ideal Characteristics

- They should feel soft on skin and go on evenly when applied.
- Line drawn should be thin and clear.
- They should be stable.
- No sweating, blooming, breakage or crumbling.

Formulation of Eyebrow Pencil

Crayon pencil is similar to lip pencil but contain higher proportion of waxes to increase the melting point so that can be molded into thin stick.

Extruded eyebrow pencil formulated in same manner to the crayon type, is placed in a wooden casing like ordinary pencil. Generally, eyebrow pencil is in the extruded form means it is similar to the ordinary lead pencil, it is less stable than moulded ones. Following is example of bases of eyebrow pencil.

Ingredients	Per cent of Total
Bees wax	25
Ozokerite	25
Butyl stearate	8
Lanolin	2
Castor oil	25
Liquid paraffin	15
Perfume	q.s.
Antioxidant	q.s.

Formula for eyebrow pencil is as follows:

Ingredients	Per cent of Total
Talc	15
TiO_2	5
Kaolin	15
Bees wax	10
Stearic acid	15
Hydrogenated castor oil	10
Petrolatum	4
Lanolin oil	3
Liquid paraffin	3
Black iron oxide	20
Antioxidant	q.s.

Manufacturing of Eyebrow Pencil

Mix black iron oxide, TiO_2, Talc and Kaolin in a blender

↓

Heat the waxes and other fatty materials

↓

Add powder mixture to molten wax

↓

Knead thoroughly to mix pigments uniformly

↓

Mold into lead and put into wooden casing

Evaluation

- Shade
- Texture
- Spredability
- Wear application
- Stability (temperature should be 40-45°C)
- Penetration.

❖❖❖

CHAPTER 7...

DENTAL CARE COSMETICS

7.1 INTRODUCTION

Both dental caries and periodontal disease can be traced to the formation of bacterial plaque on the exterior surface of the teeth. The formation of this layer rapidly follows the formation of the pellicle. Most people brush their teeth twice daily with toothpaste and many of us even supply this with a mouthwash. There is no doubt that the general knowledge regarding toothpastes and mouthwashes often come from commercials. We have all seen the commercials that shows us handsome people with flashy white smiles. The commercials want us to believe that certain toothpaste can give the consumers whiter and cleaner teeth, a fresh breath, fight plaque and calculus formation and prevent gingivitis. But what the commercials fail to tell us is that what is first and foremost important is not the product that is being used but using a correct brushing action. Consequently, many people have unrealistic and high expectations to the effect of the products. But there is no doubt that brushing with toothpaste has positive effects, especially if it contains therapeutic agents such as fluoride. It is important to be aware of the fact that the main aim of toothpastes and mouthrinses is to make the tooth brushing comfortable. The best advice to the consumers is to underline the importance of brushing with toothpaste at least once a day using a soft bristled toothbrush and a correct brushing action.

Toothpaste is defined as a semi-aqueous material for removing naturally occurring deposits from teeth and is supposed to be used simultaneous with a toothbrush.

Requirements of a Toothpaste/Dentifrice

1. When used properly, with an efficient toothbrush, it should clean the teeth adequately, that is, remove food debris, plaque and stains.
2. It should leave the mouth with a fresh, clean sensation.
3. Its cost should be such as to encourage regular and frequent use by all.
4. It should be harmless, pleasant and convenient to use.
5. It should be capable of being packed economically and should be stable in storage during its commercial shelf-life.
6. It should conform to accepted standards in terms of its abrasivity to enamel and dentine.
7. Claims should be substantiated by properly conducted clinical trials.

Main Components of Toothpastes

1. Polishing agents /abrasives (20 - 50%)
2. Detergents/Surfactant (cleaning and foaming) (1 - 3%)
3. Humectants (20 - 35%)
4. Thickening/Binding (gelling) agents (1 - 2%)
5. Sweetener
6. Flavouring agents
7. Minor ingredients (colours, whitening agents, preservatives etc.)

1. Polishing agent/ Abrasives

Abrasives which are also known as polishing agents are used to remove debris and residual stain from the teeth and for polishing the tooth surface. The commonly used abrasive includes precipitated calcium carbonate, tribasic calcium phosphate, calcium pyrophosphate, Mg trisilicate etc.

(i) Surface active agent (Detergent)

These are added to enhance the action of polishing agent by wetting the teeth, the food particle if any and to emulsify the mucous. Detergents lower the surface tension of the liquid environment in the oral cavity so that the substances in the toothpaste/mouthwash can contact the teeth more easily. They penetrate and dissolve plaque. This makes it easier to clean the teeth. The foaming effect produced by the detergent is also beneficial in cleaning the teeth and contributes to remove debris and gives a feeling of cleanness. Another function of the detergent is to help in dispersing the flavours in the toothpaste/mouthwash. For example: Dioctyl sodium, SLS soap can also be used for this purpose, but to a lesser extent due to incompatibility with calcium salt and flavouring agent.

(ii) Humectants

Humectants are added to toothpaste which will not allow the paste to become dry. The most commonly used humectants are glycerin, sorbitol and propylene glycol. Glycerin is sweet in taste and is regarded as the best humectants.

(iii) Binder

A binder is added to keep the solid and liquid in the united form and also to maintain consistency. Glycerol, sorbitol, polyethylene glycol (PEG), propylene glycol and cellulose gum are common water binding substances. Apart, gum tragacanth, gum karaya, sodium alginate, tragacanth etc. is a natural product with similar properties.

(iv) Sweetening agent

A sweetening agent is added to dentifrices to impart sweet taste to the preparation. Sorbitol, glycerin and sodium saccharine (0.005-2.5%) are most commonly used.

(v) Flavouring agent

It is one of the most important ingredients and its selection is also very important because choice of flavour varies from individual to individual. For example: peppermint, wintergreen, eucalyptus, menthol, cinnamon etc. are often used.

(vi) Preservatives

The moisture of carbohydrates presents in toothpaste lead to bacterial growth. So a preservative should be included in toothpaste to preserve its quality and stability. For example: methyl paraben, propyl paraben. Sodium benzoate is not used in toothpaste as preservative.

7.2 TOOTHPASTES

General Formulation

Ingredients	Per cent of Total
Abrasives	40.0-60
Detergents/Foaming index	1.50-3
Humectants	5-30
Binding agents	0.50-2.50
Sweetening and Flavouring agents	0.50-3
Miscellaneous ingredients	0.15-0.50

Ingredient	Formula Per cent (by weight)	Examples
Abrasive	10-50	SiO_2, $CaHPO_4$, Al_2O_3, $CaCO_3$, $Ca_2P_2O_7$
Surfactant	1.0-2.0	SLS
Humectants	10-30	Glycerin, Sorbitol (70%), Propylene Glycol
Gelling Agent	0.5-1.5	CMC, Carrageenan, HEC, Organic Polymers
Sweetener	0.05-0.5	Sodium Saccharin
Flavour	1.0-3.0	Spearmint, Menthol, Peppermint, Anethole,
Colour	< 1.0	Titanium Dioxide, colours, pH adjusters, Sparkles, etc.

Contd...

Ingredient	Formula Per cent (by weight)	Examples
Fluoride	< 0.5	Sodium Fluoride, Sodium Monofluorophosphate
Other 'active ingredients' added for therapeutic benefits or claims	< 10.0	Triclosan, Pyrophosphate salts, Potassium Nitrate, Strontium Chloride, Hydrogen Peroxide
Water to make	100	

Ingredients	Per cent of Total
Precipitated calcium carbonate	42.0
Glycerine	30.0
Propylene glycol	3.0
Gum tragacanth	1.2
Saccharin sodium	0.05
Sodium lauryl sulphate	1.3
Water to make	100
Flavour, chloroform, preservatives	q.s.

A part of calcium carbonate has been replaced with di-calcium phosphate and gum tragacanth has been replaced with sodium carboxy methyl cellulose.

Ingredients	Per cent of Total
Di-calcium phosphate	30.0
Precipitated calcium carbonate	15.0
Glycerine	25.0
Saccharin sodium	0.05
Sodium lauryl sulphate	1.2
Sodium carboxy methyl cellulose	1.0
Water to make	100
Flavour, chloroform, preservatives	q.s.

Gel Toothpastes

Ingredients	Per cent of Total
Silica*	20.0
Sorbitol solution (70%)	50.0
Glycerin	12.0
Sodium lauryl sulphate	1.5
Sodium carboxy methyl cellulose	1.5
Sodium saccharin	0.05
Water to make	100
Flavour, colour and preservatives	q.s.

Silica is a suitable abrasive in dentifrices containing fluoride. Though not popular, liquid form dentifrice can be prepared in water and alcohol mixture.

Ingredients	Per cent of Total
Sodium lauryl sulphate	1.0
Glycerine	6.0
Polyoxyethylene polypropylene glycol	0.5
Sodium saccharin	0.1
Ethanol	10.0
Water to make	100
Flavour, colour and preservatives	q.s.

Manufacture of Toothpastes

General Method A

Stage 1 is to carefully blend all powder components of the toothpaste together, including the gelling agents, abrasives and thickening agents. This blend is essential to avoid aggregation of the gelling agent.

Stage 2 is then to mix this blend with all the aqueous and liquid components of the paste (humectants, water) in a heavy-duty mixer. Following complete swelling of the gelling agent a homogeneous paste will be obtained.

General Method B

In **stage 1** of this process, the gelling agent is fully hydrated in the presence of sufficient water and heat if necessary. In addition all soluble salts may be added.

Stage 2 of the process is to mix the fully dispersed gel and the powders together also in a heavy-duty mixer. Following complete mixing a homogeneous paste will be obtained.

Addition of Flavour and Surfactants

In stage 3, the homogeneous paste obtained from either process must then be mixed with both the surfactant and the flavour under vacuum. This is essential in order to de-aerate the product at the final stage, otherwise a cosmetically unacceptable 'mousse' type consistency will be produced. Surface active agent is often added as late as possible in the manufacture because that will create foaming and air entrapment if caution is not taken. Equally mixing under vacuum with the added flavour could cause unnecessary loss of some flavor components that can be up to 25% of the total raw material cost of the toothpaste.

Other Toothpaste Formulations

(I) Anti-cavity (fluoride)

World Health Organization recognized that use of an appropriately fluoridated dental cream is one of the major reasons for a dramatic decline in caries. Various fluoride sources have been used throughout.

Caries Sites

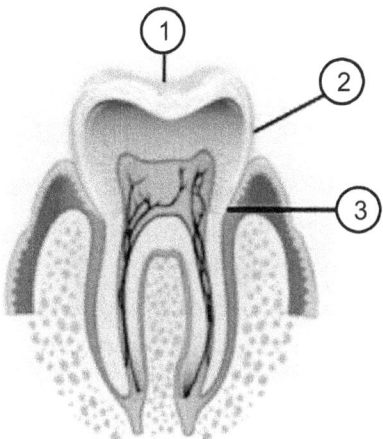

Fig. 7.1

1. **Pit-and-fissure caries** develop initially in the fissures of the teeth, but can spread into the dentine.

2. **Smooth-surface caries** are most common on inter dental surfaces, but can occur on any smooth surface of the tooth.

3. **Root caries** attack the cementum and dentine, which becomes exposed as gums recede.

Sodium Monofluorophosphate (Na_2PO_3F), Sodium Fluoride (NaF), Organo (amine) Fluorides, Stannous Fluoride (SnF_2).

Ingredient	Per cent by wt	Ingredient	Per cent by wt	Ingredient	Per cent by wt
Glycerin	22.0	Sorbitol (70%)	58.8	Glycerin	25.0
CMC	1.1	Glycerin	15.0	CMC	1.0
Na Saccharin	0.2	$NaH_2PO_4.2H_2O$	0.03	Saccharin	0.2
$Na_4P_2O_7$	0.5	$Na_2HPO_4.2H_2O$	0.2	NaMFP	0.76
NaF	0.1	Na Saccharin	0.3	Ammonium	1.9
Dicalcium Phosphate	48.0	Silica (Thickener)	3.0	Dihydrogen Phosphate	
SLS	1.5	Silica (Abrasive)	13.0	Calcium Carbonate	45.0
Flavour	0.8	SLS	1.2		
Water to make	100.0	Flavour	0.9	SLS	2.0
		NaF	0.243	Preservative	0.2
		Carbopol 940	0.3	Flavour	1.0
		Xanthan Gum	0.2	Water to make	100.0
		Water to make	100.0		

(II) Sensitivity Toothpastes

Sensitivity of the dentine is associated with the exposure of the dentine tubules, particularly around the gumline once the gingiva has receded to expose the root dentine. The most commonly used ingredients which are incorporated into a toothpaste to provide relief from sensitivity are those which are believed to block the open dentine tubules, either by deposition of mineral salts or precipitation of proteins in the tubules. These are,

- Strontium Chloride
- Strontium Acetate
- Formaldehyde

The use of soluble potassium ions as a desensitizing preparation became more prevalent. The proposed mechanism of action for these dental creams is that the soluble potassium ion can penetrate the open dentine tubules to reach the nerve fibres at the base, where it can exert a depolarizing and thus desensitizing effect. Ingredients used in these type of dental creams typically are

- Potassium Nitrate
- Potassium Chloride
- Potassium Citrate

Examples of desensitizing toothpastes are shown below.

Ingredient	Per cent by weight	Ingredient	Per cent by weight
Potassium Nitrate	10.0	Sorbitol (70%)	33.1
Glycerin	25.0	Saccharin (30%)	1.0
HEC	1.6	Strontium Acetate	8.0
Polyoxyethylene Sorbitan Monolaurate	2.0	Potassium Acetate	4.9
Silica	24.0	Sodium N-methyl-N Cocyl Laurate	2.0
Flavour	1.0	Xanthan	1.0
Na Saccharin	0.2	Glycerin	11.0
Water to make	100.0	TiO$_2$	1.0
		Silica (Thickening)	6.5
		Silica (Abrasive)	14.0
		Preservative	0.1
		Flavour	1.0
		Water to make	100.0

7.3 TOOTH POWDERS
General Formulation

Ingredients	Per cent of Total
Calcium carbonate	94
Sodium palmitate	6
Sodium saccharin	0.1
Flavour, colour and preservatives	q.s.

Ingredients	Per cent of Total
Calcium carbonate	19
Di-calcium phosphate	80
SLS	1
Sodium saccharin	0.1
Flavour, colour and preservatives	q.s.

Manufacture of Toothpowders

Ingredients in less quantity are mixed first and are mixed with remaining contents. Flavour can spray or adsorbed first on to polishing agent. This mix is screened before filling into hopper.

Evaluation of Solid Dental Products

Identification of ingredients and estimation of their contents are essential components of overall quality control and evaluation of dental care products. The products, toothpastes and tooth powders, can be basically classified into foam forming and non-foam forming.

Some Other Special Evaluation Tests are as follows:

1. **Abrasiveness:** Various tests have been designed and reported over the year, mostly on the set of extracted teeth. The teeth are mechanically brushed with pastes or powders and then the effects are studied by observation, mechanical or other means. Abrasive character normally depended on the particle size. So, study of particle size can also give such idea.

2. **Particle size:** This can be determined by microscopic study of the particles or by sieving or other means.

3. **Cleansing property:** This is studied by measuring the change in the reflectance character of a lacquer coating on the polyester film caused by brushing with a tooth cleanser (paste or powder). Also *in-vivo* test has been suggested in which teeth are brushed for two weeks and condition of teeth is assessed before and after use with the help of photographs.

4. **Consistency:** It is important that the product, paste, should maintain the consistency to enable the product press out from the container. Study of viscosity is essential for this. Rheology of powders is also important for proper flow of the powder from the container.

5. **pH of the product:** pH of the dispersion of 10% of the product in water is determined by pH meter.

6. **Foaming character:** This test is specially required for foam forming tooth pastes or tooth powders. Specific amount of product can be mixed with specific amount of water and to be shaken. The foam thus formed is studied for its nature, stability and wash ability.

7. **Limit test for arsenic and lead:** This is very important as these are highly toxic metals. Specific tests are there to estimate these two metals; products may not have excess of such metals.

8. **Volatile matters and moisture:** A specific amount of the product required to be taken in a dish and drying is to be done till constant weight. Loss of weight will indicate percentage of moisture and volatile matters.

9. **Effect of special ingredients:** Special test should be done for the special ingredients if any, like antiseptics, enzymes, etc.

7.4 MOUTHWASHES

Use of liquid dentifrices are comparatively less than solid one. They are basically aqueous or hydro alcoholic solutions of surfactants with additional components like thickening agent, sweeteners, flavours etc. Action of this preparation on dental surface is less but the cleansing effect is more. A mouthwash is defined as a non-sterile aqueous solution used mostly for its deodorant, refreshing or antiseptic effect. Mouthwashes or rinses are designed to reduce oral bacteria, remove food particles, temporary reduce bad breathe and provide a pleasant taste.

The amount of the different components in mouthwashes varies from product to product. Some practically have the same composition as toothpastes. Distinct from toothpastes most mouth rinses contain alcohol, as a preservative and a semi-active ingredient. The amount of alcohol is usually ranging from 18 – 26%. They do not contain any abrasive as they will sediment.

The important components of mouthwash are as follows:

Antiseptic Substances: Substances most commonly used are phenol and its derivatives, hexachlorophene etc.

Astringents: These are added to,

- Shrink and protect inflamed mucous surfaces.
- Precipitate proteins and saliva.
- Diminish accumulated mucous secretions by precipitations.

Zinc chlorides, zinc acetate, aluminium sulphate (alum) (all in 0.05-0.2%) are commonly used.

Deodorizing Agent: Quaternary ammonium compounds, chlorophyllin have been found to exert Deodorizing effect in oral cavity.

Formulation

Ingredients	Per cent of Total
Sodium myristate sulphate	4.0
Methyl cellulose	4.0
Saccharine sodium	0.1
Flavours	0.3
Glycerin	5.0
Alcohol	10.0
Water to make	100

Requirements of a Mouthwash

The primary function of a mouthwash, like that of a dentifrice, is to freshen the mouth and breathe by swishing/swilling the product around the mouth, followed by expectoration (spitting out).

It achieves this by a combination of three factors:

- The mechanical effect of rinsing debris from the mouth.
- The effect of the flavour.
- The effect of any agent specifically added to deliver the required end benefit (e.g. anti-bacterial).

Fluoride and Other Active Ingredients

Obviously, nearly all therapeutic ingredients used in toothpastes have been used in mouthwash if they are water soluble. This includes Fluoride, Pyrophosphate ions, Triclosan, Chlorhexidene, Cetyl Pyridinium Chloride, Hydrogen Peroxide, Potassium ions and others.

Anti-cavity Mouthwash

Ingredient	Per cent of Total
Alcohol	5.0
Glycerin	7.5
Sorbitol (75%)	7.5
Plutonic F127	1.0
Pluronic F108	1.0
Na Saccharin	0.02
NaF	0.05
Flavour	0.08
Water to make	100

Evaluation

1. Antiseptic properties
2. *In-vitro* Antiseptic properties
3. *In-vivo* Antiseptic properties
4. Deodorizing effect
5. Stability etc.

CHAPTER **8**

MANICURE PRODUCTS

8.1 INTRODUCTION

The nail lacquers are the largest and most important group of manicure preparations. It is also known as nail enamel or nail varnish. The application of nail lacquers covers the nail with water and air impermeable membrane which remains for days and normally can be removed only by suitable solvent. Film should be continuous and must adhere to the nail surface, it should not peel off. The film should be glossy and must retain the gloss under the influence of external interfering factors such as humidity, air, light, warm or cold, soap and detergent solutions.

Nails are transparent protective coverings on finger tips and toes of feet. The care of nails is referred to as Manicuring.

Manicure preparations includes:

- Nail lacquer/enamel/paint/varnish
- Enamel remover
- Powder polish
- Nail cream
- Nail bleach
- Cuticle remover
- Cuticle softener.

8.2 NAIL LACQUERS

"Nail lacquers are viscous preparations intended to decorate nails of fingers and toes".

The characters of the film are expected to be as follows:

1. It should be of even thickness for which viscosity should be proper and satisfactory.
2. It should have good gloss.
3. Good adhesion to the nail.
4. Satisfactory flexibility to avoid brittleness and cracking.
5. It should form a non-tacky surface.
6. Quick drying character.
7. Long maintenances of the film character.

A good lacquer base is a blend of various components like:

1. Film Formers

The common film former for nail lacquers is nitrocellulose or cellulose nitrate. The other film formers used are cellulose acetate, cellulose acetobutyrate, ethyl cellulose and methacrylate and vinyl resins. Nitrocellulose film is better in terms of hardness, toughness, resistance to abrasion and low solvent retention capacity. Films of nitrocellulose are waterproof and stable to atmospheric conditions.

The solubility of nitrocellulose depends on the degree of nitration of cellulose. There are three grades of nitrocellulose based on degree of nitration. The SS grade contains the lowest degree of nitrogen (10.9-11.2%). It is soluble in esters, ketones and glycol ethers and can tolerate significant amounts of hydrocarbons and lower alcoholic solvents. Due to its higher hydroxyl content, the SS grade is sensitive to moisture. The middle grade of nitration is called AS grade and the RS grade contains the highest degree of nitration (11.8-12.2%). RS grade nitrocellulose is typically used in nail lacquers. RS type nitrocellulose is soluble in esters, ketones and glycol ethers. It can tolerate small amounts of alcohol and hydrocarbons. Since, it contains lower amounts of hydroxyl groups, it is the least water sensitive grade of nitrocellulose.

The molecular weight of nitrocellulose affects solution viscosity. The viscosity of a nitrocellulose solution is measured by the "falling ball" method. The viscosity is measured by the time taken for a steel ball of specific size and density to travel a given distance in a solution of nitrocellulose of known concentration in a specific solvent mixture. Lower viscosity solutions have lower molecular weight and shorter times required for the steel ball to descend.

Nitrocellulose degrades when exposed to heat, sunlight, alkaline materials and some metals, especially iron. Therefore, it is important to store nitrocellulose in a non-ferrous lined sealed container.

2. Resins

Resins are incorporated in nail lacquers to give the film more body, gloss, depth and adhesion. It also helps in dispersing insoluble pigments and lakes. The natural resins such as dammar, benzoin, sandarac, shellac and ester gum etc. The synthetic resins, sulphonamide, formaldehyde resins are presently used most.

3. Plasticizers

Plasticizers are used in the formulation to impact flexibility and adhesive properties to the film. Nitrocellulose or other film formers alone, make a dull and brittle film which can easily flake off the nail. It should be colourless, odourless and non-toxic.

Types of Plasticizers are as follows:

(a) Solvent plasticizers

These are the solvents for nitrocellulose and they are high molecular weight esters having fairly high B.P. and low volatility. Example: Butyl acetyl recinolate.

(b) Non-solvent plasticizers

These are not a solvent for nitrocellulose and are not compatible with nitrocellulose. These cannot be used alone. Example: Castor oil if used in proportion of 1 : 1 it produce flexible film. Formulation may contain one, two or sometime more than two plasticizers. Examples: Dibutyl phthalate, phosphates, glycol late, sulphonamides and citrate. Good plasticizers should have the following characters:

(i)   Miscible with other ingredients.
(ii) Non-irritating and non-toxic.
(iii) Low volatility
(iv) Improve flexibility, gloss and adhesion
(v) Colourless, odourless and stable.

4. Solvents

Solvents are volatile organic liquids that combine all ingredients of lacquers and make a homogenous viscous preparation. Evaporation is the main characteristics of solvents and it depends upon specific heat, latent heat of evaporation, molecular weight etc. Too rapid rate of evaporation causes poor flow of lacquer resulting in uneven and streaky applications. Very quickly evaporating solvents may cause intense cooling; this causes precipitation of moisture from surrounding atmosphere making the film dull with unattractive finish. This is called blushing of lacquers.

Solvents are generally classified according to boiling point:

(a) Low boiling point solvents - Ethyl ether, petroleum ether, acetone, cyclohexane
(b) Medium boiling point solvents - N-butyl acetate, amyl acetate, n-butyl alcohol
(c) High boiling point solvents - Ethyl lactate, butyl cellulose.

Usually, a mixture of solvents is used to give desired characteristics. Solvents can be placed into three inter-related categories:

(i) Active solvents: These solvents are referred to as *active solvents* as they actively dissolve the polar nitrocellulose (the main film-forming polymer) and modifiers used in nail lacquers. Hydrocarbon solvents consist of only carbon and hydrogen and they lack oxygen. They are referred to as *diluents* as they do not dissolve the film-former or the modifier by themselves but are often added to lower the cost of the formulation. N-butyl acetate, propyl acetate and ethyl acetate are the most commonly used ester solvents in typical nail lacquer formulations.

(ii) Couples: These are the non-solvent for nitrocellulose but when used in conjunction they increase the strength of active solvent.

(iii) Diluents: They are not exactly solvents but are organic solvents miscible with nitrocellulose solvents. Diluents are incorporated for multiple purposes.

• These are the non-solvent for nitrocellulose
• These are used to stabilize viscosity, to carry resins in solution.

- Aromatic and aliphatic hydrocarbons, alcohols are commonly used diluents. Alcohols are very efficient diluents.
- Butyl alcohol (evaporation is optimum but tend to lower the viscosity of NC solution)
- Isopropyl alcohol (widely used because of low cost and easy availability) the aromatic hydrocarbons tend to increase viscosity of NC solution and also tend to impart poor flow property.

5. Pigments

Impart acceptable shade to the lacquer base.

(a) These should be non-toxic and non-irritating.

(b) These should be non-staining.

(c) These should be compatible with other ingredients of lacquers.

(d) These should be insoluble in lacquers.

(e) These should be moderately stable when exposed to light.

The soluble dyes like erythrosine, carmosine and rhodomines are used but are found to stain skin so they are not used. Inorganic pigments are titanium dioxide, yellow iron oxide, red iron oxide, iron blue, iron black, chromoxide green etc.

6. Other Formulating Agents

(i) **Suspending agents:** Suspending properties have been achieved by developing thixotropic system using pre-heated colloidal clays. Examples, Benzyl dimethyl hydrogenated tallow, Ammonium montmorillonite (Bentone 27), Dimethyl dioctadecyl ammonium bentonite (Bentone 34).

(ii) **Opacifying agents:** These are whitening agents which help to develop shades which will reflect the same colour on the nails as they are in the bottle.

Examples, Titanium dioxide, Zinc oxide.

(iii) **UV absorbers:** To prevent deterioration of ingredients due to UV light.

Examples, Benzophenones and its derivatives.

(iv) **Perfume:** Used mainly to counteract the unpleasant odour of the solvents. Synthetic perfumes are preferred.

In practice, we required 2-3 coats or applications:

(a) Base coats

(b) Nail lacquer base (as mention earlier)

(c) Top coats

(a) Base Coats

To prepare the nail for better acceptance of the enamel, base coats have been developed. These contain higher quantities of resin to increase adhesion and quick drying solvents. A lower non-volatile content and lower viscosity is desirable.

Formula 1

Ingredients	Per cent of Total
Nitrocellulose	18.5
Dibutyl phthalate	3
Santolite MS 80	6.5
Ethyl acetate	10
Butyl acetate	25
Isopropyl alcohol	10
Toluene	27

Formula 2

Ingredients	Per cent of Total
Nitrocellulose	18.5
Santolite MS 80	6.5
Dibutyl phthalate	2
Ethyl alcohol	5
Ethyl acetate	34
Toluene	39

Mixture of ethyl alcohol and toluene is used to obtain optimum viscosity of NC solution. Further addition of castor oil or liquid acetylated monoglyceride impart additional plasticizing effect and make the film longer lasting with less tendency to chip.

Dissolve NS in solvent mix.

↓

Add santolite and dibutyl phthalate

↓

Mix homogenously

Top Coats

For increased thickness of film, greater luster and resistance to abrasion and wear, top coats are applied. Formulation contain higher per cent of NC and plasticizer, lower per cent of resin and higher per cent of diluents.

Ingredients	Per cent of Total
Nitrocellulose	16
Santolite	4
Dibutyl phthalate	5
Ethyl/Isopropyl alcohol	10
Ethyl acetate	10
Butyl acetate	10
Toluene	45

Pigments (3-5%) are usually added in the solution to the lacquers base to prepare final product.

The manufacture of nail enamels involves following distinct processes,

- Grinding of pigments
- Manufacture of Nail lacquers
- Mixing of pigments with lacquer
- Safety aspects

Add 75% of the solvent and whole of the diluents in a mixer. Mix well with agitation

↓

Nitrocellulose is then added with stirrer on

↓

Solvent is added

↓

Plasticizer is added

↓

Resin is added

↓

Mixing is continued for several hours until solution of all ingredients is complete

↓

Clear lacquer is formed

↓

Passed through filter press or centrifuged

↓

Pigmented chips added and mixing is continued

↓

Nail lacquer product is formed

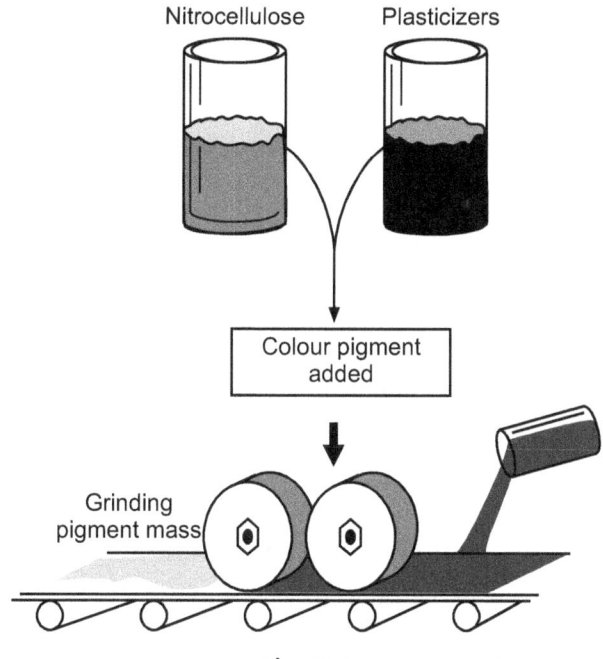

Fig. 8.1

Cream Type Enamels

These materials are available as concentrated dispersions in enamel base and can be blended with lacquer for desired effect.

Frosted Nail Enamel

These are prepared by incorporating frosted nail enamel concentrates. These are viscous NC pastes contain NH_4^+ modified clay as thixotropic agent. On dilution with clear lacquers, non-setting pearlescent nail enamel is obtained.

Pearl concentrates are based on:

1. Synthetic pearl (Bismuth oxychloride)
2. Natural pearl essence (Guanine).

Paste concentrates containing 25% pigments are also available with given stable enamel on diluting with suspending lacquer. Stabilization of bismuth oxychloride is required as may darken in UV radiation.

Formulation of a Pearlescent Nail lacquer

Ingredients	Per cent of Total
Nitrocellulose	1.5
Butyl acetate	25
Ethyl acetate	12
Toulene	25

Toulene sulphonamide formaldehyde resin	10
Dibutyl phthalate	5
Camphor	2
Stearakonium hectorite	1
Benzophenone-1	0.20
D & C Red No. 7, Calcium lake	q.s.
D & C, Red. No. 34, Calcium Lake	q.s.
FD&C, No. 5, Aluminium lake	q.s.
Bismuth oxychloride (25%)	5.00
Iron oxides	0.15

Filling

Since, nail lacquers are highly inflammable, filling, capping and packing must be carried out under fire-proof and explosion-proof conditions. Proper care and precautions should be followed, for example, good ventilation, proper electrical wiring and prohibition of cigarette smoking in the working area.

Packing and Labeling

Glass bottles with a brush applicator are the most conventional container which is used for the packaging of nail lacquers. The capacity varies from 8 ml to 18 ml. The applicator consists of an air-tight aluminium canister with an acrylic fibre tip or nib which applies polish directly to nails.

Fig. 8.2: Bottles

Evaluation

Before nail lacquer is packed, the following tests should be carried out as a measure of quality control:

(a) Colour: The colour of each batch is compared with master colour standards, by applying standard colour on one nail and product on another.

(b) Drying time: Apply a film of sample under controlled conditions. Note the time required to form dry to touch film (the film may be touched with a clear finger tip without the resultant transfer of any material to the finger.

(c) Smoothness: Film form by the product should not show any foreign matter or coat particles and should be free from orange peel effect.

(d) Gloss: Can be observed visually or using reflection of light.

(e) Hardness: The film can be cast on glass plate, initially dried at 25°C (48 hours) followed by 70°C (2 hours) and conditioned at 25°C. It is then scratch with nail to test hardness.

(f) Application properties: It is check by actual application on nails.

(g) Viscosity: Brookfield viscometers are used.

8.3 LACQUER REMOVER

Nail removers / nail cleansers are defined as the mixture of solvents containing small amounts of fat intended to remove the nail enamel.

An ideal lacquer remover should have the following characteristics:

- It should not be too volatile to evaporate during application.
- It should not be irritating to surrounding skin.
- It should not leave the nails fatty or sticky.
- It should not have strong degreasing effect to leave nails brittle.
- It should not have unpleasant and obstructive odour.

Formulations

Volatile solvents (acetone, ethyl acetate, and toluene) cause dehydration and removes natural fat from nails. Hence, to avoid this solvent blends or addition of oily materials (castor, almond oil, olive, cotton seed, and mineral oil) is carried out. All safety precautions should be observed in manufacturing of enamel removers.

Types and Formulation of Enamel Removers

Type 1: Contains solvent blends and a small percentage of oily materials.

Ingredients	Per cent of Total
Castor oil	2.5
Diethylene glycol mono ethyl ether	14.5
Acetone	83.0

Type 2: (Non-smearing enamel) Contains water and water miscible solvents.

Ingredients	Per cent of Total
Water	10.0
Ethyl acetate	90.0

Type 3: (Cream type enamel remover) contains solvent, waxes and soap.

Ingredients	Per cent of Total
Bees wax	3.0
Micro-crystalline wax	1.0
Acetylated monoglycerides	10.0
Diethylene glycol monoethyl ether	52.0
Ethyl acetate	15.0
Stearic acid	15.0
Triethanolamine	4.0

Method of Preparation

Melt all ingredients except triethanolamine, add triethanolamine to the mixture with stirring and allow cooling.

Type 4: (Gel type varnish remover) contains hydroxy propyl cellulose.

Ingredients	Per cent of Total
Hydroxy propyl cellulose	1.0
Butyrol acetone	75.0
PPG-12-PEG-50 lanolin	1.0
Pigment (in Butyrol acetone)	0.1
Sodium hydroxide (5% aqueous)	q.s.
Water to make	100.0

Preparation: Mix all except hydroxyl propyl cellulose and form of well agitated liquid at R.T. then add cellulose slow enough to permit particles to separate in liquid. However, all the powder should be added before appreciable viscosity build up is obtained. Disperse for 10 minutes and then allows wet for 30 minutes. Then stir for 5 minutes.

Type 5: (Conditioning nail polish remover) Contains Malleated Soyabean oil and acetone.

Ingredients	Per cent of Total
Malleated Soyabean oil	10.0
Acetone	90.0

CHAPTER 9

BABY COSMETICS

9.1 INTRODUCTION

Babies are blessed with a skin that has not withstood any of the damage caused by years of exposure to the element. But this means that this skin is delicate. That is why it is important to clean and moisturize this skin with only mildest soap, lotion, oil and powders.

Instead of using ingredients that are potentially harmful, we must use gentle natural ingredients to ensure safety of baby's skin.

Certain wide range variety of baby products is:

1. Baby oil
    (a) Baby massage oil
    (b) Baby scalp oil
    (c) Baby hair oil
2. Baby Powders
3. Baby Soap (cleaning agent)
4. Baby Shampoo (cleaning agent)

Baby's skin plays an important role in maintaining health and if proper oils are used for massage then their skin acts against irritants, toxins and become a defending agent.

General skin problems which are often observed in babies are:

*   Baby's skin is 10 times thinner than adult skin hence has a tendency to loose moisture easily.
*   Babies often have dry skin because there oil secretary gland are not fully developed.

Hence, there is need of baby oil which cleans and moisturizes baby skin effectively without removing baby's natural oil.

9.2 BABY OIL

(a) Baby Massage Oil

Ideal properties of baby massage oil are as follows:

*   It should have ability to moisturize baby's delicate skin and help to protect from dryness.
*   It should soothe and relieve dry, rough patches.
*   It should be mild and gentle.

- Fast absorbing ability along with spread-ability.
- Skin should retain elasticity without feeling greasy.

Safety precautions are as follows:

- It should use externally.
- Do not apply on irritated skin.
- If rashes occur discontinue the use.

Formulation

Ingredients	Per cent of Total
White mineral oil	45.5
Refined arachis oil (peanut oil)	54.2
Oxyquinoline benzoate	0.2
Malein anhydride	0.1

Infant massage oil is beneficial in many ways:

- Relay from pain.
- Use in severe abdominal pain, usually of fluctuating severity. It is common among babies due to gas in intestine associated with feeding difficulties. (partial obstruction of intestine)
- Ease muscle spasm (involuntary muscular contraction).
- Stimulation of sense of touch.
- Increase blood flow.
- Promote growth and development of baby.

Evaluation

1. Dermal toxicity
2. Allergic reaction
3. Peroxide value: If peroxides value is more, chances of instability, discoloration, rancidity are more. Certain environmental conditions like high temperature, light, oxygen are also responsible. The number of peroxidase present is an index of its primary oxidation level and consequence of its tendency to undergo rancidity.

(b) Baby Scalp Oil

Ideal properties of scalp oil:

- It must be light.
- Non-staining.
- Poses conditioning properties.
- It should not be too viscous.
- It should show calming effect.

- It prevent the flaking of soft skin from skin.

Ingredients	Per cent of Total
Olive oil	91.40
Steavea seed oil	8.5
Perfume	q.s.
Chloro thymol	0.1

Certain aloe vera extracts, vitamin B_5 (nourishes hair roots and strengthen them), coconut oil, olive oil, almond oil are also preferred. Evaluation parameters are similar to massage oil. Baby scalp oil is really good moisturizer as it works well on baby scalp when they get cradle cap. It is one of the common skin problems. It is seborrhea dermatitis caused by overactive sebaceous gland, a natural build-up of cells due to hormonal changes. Homeopathy remedy include applying lozenges containing menthol/zinc.

9.3 BABY POWDERS

Baby powders are the preparations which are applied on babies face/ body by powder puffs. It provides visual covering to the skin and imparts smooth finish to it.

Qualities of good baby powders are:

- It should be very fine and should not have gritty particles.
- It should be non-toxic, non-irritant.
- It should not remove from the skin immediately after its application.
- It must be stable both physically and chemically.
- It should have good absorbing property of excess of oil and moistures.
- It should conceal shine and minor infections.
- It must be capable to keep skin smooth and soft.

Warnings to use baby powder:

- Use externally.
- Close tightly after use.
- Do not use on broken skin.
- Avoid contact with eyes.
- Apply powder with the help of powder puff.

Formula 1

Ingredients	Per cent of Total
Talc	75
Magnesium Stearate	15
Kaolin	10
Perfume	q.s.

Formula 2

Ingredients	Per cent of Total
Talc	72
Magnesium Stearate	6
Kaolin	20
Glyceryl stearate	1
Cetyl alcohol	1
Perfume	q.s.

Formula 3

Ingredients	Per cent of Total
Talc	90
Magnesium Stearate	5
Starch	5
Perfume	q.s

General Method of Preparation

All the solid ingredients are powdered and pass through sieve 120 and mix thoroughly, then incorporate required quantity of perfume.

Certain compression agents (like microcrystalline cellulose/polyethylene) are used in case of dustless baby powder. Emollients, lubricant are also used.

Talc used in most of the formulation has certain advantages and disadvantages. Talc is mineral containing hydrated magnesium stearates. It is inorganic, naturally occurring mineral talc (Magnesium silicate hydroxide).

Talc powder contains combination of zinc stearates, magnesium silicate, which are finely ground. The size of the particles is so small that they are easily inhaled and can reach the lungs (causing inflammation, swelling), extreme cases pneumonia.

In industries, the powder is sifted so as to obtain minimum size. Then, it is passed through a mill that grinds powders to a specific micro size.

Air spinning process (for obtaining bulk powder): A powder is whirled around by a purified air stream under pressure. Thus, causes powder particles to be knocked against one another at increased speed. Due to this process fine powder is obtained leads to uniform distribution of colour and perfume.

Evaluation

- Dermatological test.
- Allergy test.

- Determination of safety and efficacy by using infant as volunteers and noting their score after 1 and half month.

0	No erythemia
1	Very slight erythema
2	Well erythema
3	Moderate to severe erythema
4	Severe erythema

- Particle size (by using microscope / sieve analysis).
- Density of powder.
- Stability testing.
- Shade control and lightning - compare powder sample with standard, spread out on a white paper background.
- Dispersion of colour - No segregation must be observed. Spread powder on white paper and check it with magnifying glass.
- Pay-off - Adhesion with the puff of powder, increase pressure will make cake so hard that powder will not rub on the cake easily enough. There will be insufficient adhesion of material to the puff. Decrease pressure will make cake so soft that will find to be crumble and break.
- Flow properties by determining angle of repose.

9.4 BABY SOAP

Baby's skin is very sensitive, delicate and hence can get easily damaged and with their developing immune system, babies are more likely to get an infection. Hence, we can prevent this by keeping skin clean and clear.

Ideal properties of baby soap are:

- It should not sting baby's eyes (initially babies do not have normal tear secretions) that protect their eyes from irritation. This blinking process is also not rapid that defend from foreign matters.
- It should help to maintain specific level of moisture. Thin skin hence loosens moisture.
- It should help to preserve skin oil.
- Soap should have ability to clean babies' skin effectively without removing baby's natural oils.
- It must be helpful to treat eczema, superficial inflammation of the skin mainly affecting epidermis.

Ingredients used in baby soap are:

- Oils: Olive oil, coconut oil, palm oil, castor oil, sunflower oil etc.
- Glycerin (emollient)
- NaOH (saponifying agent)
- Sorbitol (moisturizer)
- Shea butter, cocoa butter, Sorbitan oleate (emulsifier)
- Soya bean (conditioner)
- TiO_2 (whitener) and
- Fragrance.

Evaluation

- Dermatological test
- Allergy test
- Skin irritation test on animals.

9.5 BABY SHAMPOOS

This is one of the cleaning products. Baby shampoos are the preparations which contain surface active agents. They are used to clean up cradle cap. It is also help to remove dust, grease from the hair, scalp without affecting natural gloss of hair. Baby's hair is very thin, soft and sensitive. Hence, ingredients used in the shampoo should not cause any harm to their hair. Certain wide range of non-tears shampoo is available due to which eyes of the babies are protected from harmful substances. Shampoo must be such that it will not affect the babies hair, keep them soft lustrous.

Properties of Ideal Shampoos

- It must be capable of washing away the flakes along with dandruff on the scalp gently.
- It must be non-toxic, non-irritant.
- It should provide light aroma after first use.
- It should get easily removed by washing with water.
- It should not absorb the total moisture present in the scalp and making it dry.
- Less irritating to the eyes.

Formulation of Shampoos

- Wide range of surfactant (non-ionic) are much preferred as they are milder than charge anionic. Shampoos containing oat extract, SLS in baby shampoo along with lather cleansers that cleans without drying because it is soap free.
- Conditioning agents are used to lubricate the hair and improves the texture of the hair. It smoothen the hair. It makes the hair soft and shiny. For example: lanoline, glycerin, propylene glycol.
- Thickening agents are used to increase the viscosity of shampoos and to provide consistency. For example: polyvinyl alcohol, methyl cellulose, sodium alginate, stearates.

- Solubilizing agents are used for solubilizing poorly soluble substances so as to get a clear shampoo. For example: ethyl alcohol, glycerol, PG, diethylene glycol.
- Opacifying agents are used to make shampoos opaque. For example: glyceryl stearates, stearic amides, glycerol.
- Preservatives are used to preserve shampoos against bacteria and mould contamination. For example: methyl and propyl paraben.

Direction to Use

1. Wet the hair with lukewarm water
2. Apply shampoo gently
3. Form a lather
4. Rinse

There is difference between child and adult hairs. They differ in texture, density and colour. If the nature of baby hair is curly initially before washing detangle them. We can use mild shampoo/dilute to strength.

Hard water (ground well water) must be avoided as it may fade colour of babies hair, loss of shine and thin. Use of hard water may lead to excess dryness and may also clog hair follicles that cause flakes, dry scalp.

Choice of shampoo based on,

- Choose the shampoo depending upon the type of hair/ nature of hair.
- pH rating: alkaline shampoo is stronger but harshes on hair, it may make it brittle.
- Choose a shampoo whose pH is between 5-6.8.
- Shampoos containing citric, lactic and phosphoric acid have high pH but this can be used by diluting the shampoo.

Clear Liquid Shampoo

Ingredients	Per cent of Total	Role
Miranol	30.00	Solubilizing and thickening agent
Hexylene glycol	2	Conditioning agent
Tween 20	1	Viscosity builder
Water to make	100	Vehicle

Evaluation

- Dermatologic test.
- If irritation occurs tested on animals.
- After foaming and lathering properties are analyzed along with rheologic properties.

CHAPTER 10...

COSMECEUTICALS

INTRODUCTION

Cosmeceuticals are future generation of skin care. They are the advances made within the world of dermatological products and the new backbone in skin care. Cosmeceuticals are topical cosmetic pharmaceutical hybrids intended to enhance the health and beauty of skin. Some cosmeceuticals are naturally derived while others are synthetic; but all contain functional ingredients with either therapeutic, disease fighting or healing properties.

The cosmeceuticals are topical agents distributed across a broad spectrum of materials lying somewhere among pure cosmetics (lipstick and rouge) and pure drugs (antibiotics, corticosteroids). Cosmeceuticals improve appearance, but they do so by delivering nutrients necessary for healthy skin.

- It represents a relationship between cosmetics and pharmaceuticals.
- They are topically applied but contain ingredients that influence biological function of skin.
- They claim to improve skin tone, texture and radiance while reducing wrinkling.
- They are not subject to review by F and D administration and term cosmeceuticals not recognized by Federal Food, Drug and Cosmetic Act.
- They are fastest growing segment of natural personal care industry.

10.1 REGULATORY STATUS OF COSMECEUTICALS

Cosmeceuticals - cosmetics or drugs?

The legal difference between a cosmetic and a drug is determined by a product's intended use. Under present concept, the boundary at which a cosmetic product becomes drug is not well-defined and different laws and regulations apply to each type of product.

The drugs and cosmetics Act 1940 defines a drug and a cosmetic as;

Drug: "All medicines for internal or external use of human beings or animals and all substances intended to be used for or in the diagnosis, treatment, mitigation or prevention of any disease or disorder in humans or animals".

Cosmetic: "Any article intended to be rubbed, poured, sprinkled or sprayed on or introduced into or applied to any part of the human body for cleansing, beautifying, promoting attractiveness or altering the appearance and includes any article intended for use as a component of cosmetic".

Cosmetic and Drug: Some products meet the definitions of both cosmetics and drugs. This may happen when a product has more than one intended uses. For example, a shampoo is a cosmetic because its intended use is to clean the hair. An antidandruff shampoo is a drug because its intended use is to treat dandruff. Among the cosmetic/drug combinations, toothpastes contains fluoride, deodorants that are antiperspirants and moisturizers with sun-protection claims. The claims made about drugs are subject to detailed analysis by the Food and Drug Administration (FDA) review and approval process, but cosmetics are not subject to mandatory FDA review. Although there is no legal category called cosmeceuticals, the term has found application to designate the products at the borderline between cosmetics and pharmaceuticals.

Federal Food, Drug and Cosmetic Act do not recognize the term itself. It is also often difficult for consumers to determine whether 'claims' about the actions or efficiency of cosmeceuticals are valid unless the product has been approved by the FDA or equivalent agency. Some countries have the classes of products that fall between the two categories of cosmetics and drugs: for example, Japan has 'Quasi-drugs'; Thailand has 'controlled cosmetics' and Hong Kong has 'cosmetic-type drugs'. The regulations of cosmeceuticals have not been harmonized between the USA, European, Asian and other countries.

10.2 HISTORY OF COSMECEUTICALS

Raymond Reed, founder of the U.S. Society of cosmetic chemists, created the concept of "cosmeceutical" in 1961. Further the term '"cosmeceutical" was popularized by American dermatologist Albert Kligman in the late 1970s. However, the Egyptians were the first to recognize the health giving properties of cosmetics. The "Ebers" a medical papyrus wrote in 1600 EC, made frequent reference to several cosmeceutical type products. A favorite formulation was using honey and milk that claimed to help cure skin diseases. This phenomenon occurred when the modern pharmaceutical industry was first developed and the first government statute regulating the sale of drugs was drafted.

10.3 COSMECEUTICAL AGENTS

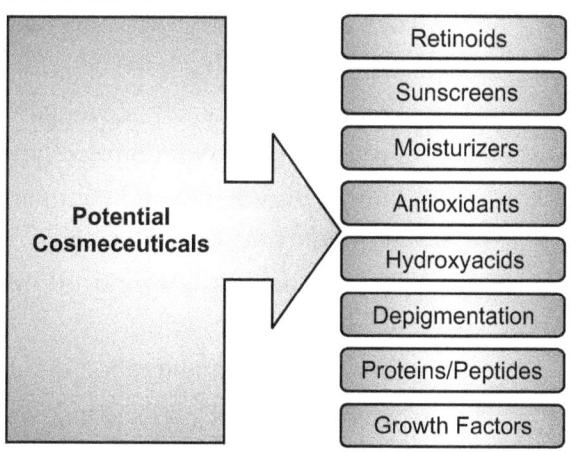

Mechanism of Action of Cosmeceuticals

The modem cosmeceutical products act functionally. However ten basic mechanism of action of cosmeceuticals are,

Cosmeceutical	Function
Retinoids	- Antioxidants and activate specific genes and proteins
α-Hydroxy acids	- Increase epidermal exfoliation and increase dermal collagen deposition
Antioxidants	- Neutralize free radicals and protect cell membranes
Vitamin C	- Antiaging potential, inhibits melanogenesis and promotes collagen synthesis
Vitamin E	- Moisturizing effect and weak photoprotective potential
Panthenol	- Humectants
Lipoic acid	- Able to recycle other antioxidants
Ubiquinone (coenzyme Q10)	- Exhibits antiapoptotic activity and inhibits the expression of collagenase
Niacinamide	- Antitumor activity; promotes increased epidermal turnover and exfoliation
Dimethylaminoethanol	- Improves skin firmness and lift sagging skin; diminishes cross-linking of proteins
Spin traps	- Interact with reactive free radicals and augment the effect of antioxidant enzymes
Melatonin	- Yields antimutagenic, UV-protective and oncostatic effects
Catalase	- Imparts antioxidative activity in the skin
Glutathione	- Antioxidant
Superoxide dismutase	- Decreases UV erythema and damage
Peroxidase	- Additional antibacterial activity
Glycopyranosides	- Potent free-radical scavengers with further cardio protection and neuro protection
Polyphenols	- Inhibit UV induced tumorigenesis; reduce UV erythema and sunburn cells
Cysteine	- Protects against UV-induced immune suppression and tumorigenesis
Allantoin	- Promotes cell proliferation and healing process
Furfuryl adenine	- Acts as a growth factor, increases epidermal thickness and collagen synthesis

Uric acid	-	Has a sparing action in plasma ascorbate
Carnosine	-	Has also metal ion-scavenging activities
Depigmenting agents	-	Inhibit melanogenesis at different stages
Botanicals	-	Exert effects through the mechanisms of antioxidants, α-hydroxy acids, etc.
Glycosamino glycans	-	Stimulate epidermal regeneration and wound healing
Anticellulites	-	Yield lipolysis
Enzymes	-	Exfoliate keratotic skin; reduce UV-induced carcinogenesis
Growth factors	-	Increases epidermal thickness and collagen synthesis; accelerate wound healing
Hormones	-	Retards skin aging through reversing skin tone and elasticity
Botulinum A exotoxin	-	Eliminates wrinkles through blocking the sympathetic muscle innervations
Peptides	-	Stimulates collagen and extracellular matrix production; yield copper in the tissues
Antimicrobical agents	-	Inhibits microorganisms and microbial decomposition in perspiration
Topical anesthetics/antipruritics	-	Relieves local discomfort and reduce pruritus
Hair removal/hair loss therapy	-	Hydrolyze and disrupt hair keratin's bonds/act like hormones
Scar management	-	Modulates collagenase kinetics

(I) Retinoid

They are most prevalent cosmeceuticals in market. They are vitamin A derivatives present in all living organism either as performed vitamin A/carotenoids. Vitamin A (retinol) is necessary for the proper growth, bone development and integrity of mucosal and epithelial surface. Eye and skin severely affected by deficiency of retinol. The useful concentration of topical retinol ranges from 0.3% to 1%. Vitamin A (retinol) is the prototype of all other retinoids and is necessary for proper growth, bone development and integrity of mucosal and epithelial surfaces. In vitamin A deficiency, the eyes and skin are severally affected.

Vitamin A exists in three isomeric forms among which beta form found to be more active than alpha and gamma isomer. Its deficiency may lead to dry rough skin. Since then, vitamin A and its derivatives have been useful in the treatment of many skin disorders, including ichthyosis, acne, and psoriasis.

(II) Hydroxyl Acids

They are organic carboxylic acid and classified into Alpha Hydroxy Acids (AHAs) and Beta Hydroxy Acids (BHAs).

Alpha Hydroxy Acids (AHAs)

- Range from simple aliphatic compound of complex molecules.
- Derived from natural sources and referred to as fruit acids.
- They includes glycolic acid, mandelic acid, lactic acid, malic acid, citric acid, tartaric acid
- Shown to decrease signs of aging.
- Skin appears smoother and more uniform.
- Enhance epidermal shedding, improve quality of elastic fibres and increase density of collagen.

Beta Hydroxy Acids (BHAs)

- BHAs are aromatic compound.
- Salicylic acid is reference BHA and has dermatolytic properties and help in xerotic and ichthyotic disorders.
- It includes 2 – hydroxyl – 5 – octanoyl benzoic acid.
- Studies shows that AHAs increases sensitivity to UV radiation and that sunscreen application may advisable when these products are used.

(III) Antioxidant

Skin frequently exposed to constant endogenous and exogenous damaging agents. UV radiation, drugs, air pollutant and heat/cold are continually challenging, protective characters of skin. Skin has to cope with endogenous microgens, Reactive O_2 Species (ROS) and other free radicals. These species continuously produced during physiological cellular metabolism. To counteract harmful effect of ROS, skin equipped with pro-oxidant/ damaging agent and antioxidant / protective agent.

They reduce free-radical damage by blocking the oxidative processes in cells. These are used to protect skin from photo damage, cancer and photoaging. Antioxidants inhibit inflammation that causes collagen depletion. They protect against photo damage and skin cancer. Some antioxidants includes vitamins A, C and E, alpha lipoic acid, lactobionic acid, ubiquinone (coenzyme Q-10), idebenone, polyphenols, catechins, flavonoids etc.

(IV) Depigmentation Agents

Hydroquinone, aloesin, arbutin, azelaic acid, glycolic acid, kojic acids are some multiple depigmentation agents. Hydroquinone is effective and widely used for treatment of melasma, post inflammatory hyperpigmentation. It acts by inhibiting conversion of tyrosine to melanin.

(V) Protein and Peptides

Cosmeceutical peptides have the potential to improve the appearance of aging skin. There are various types of cosmeceutical peptides such as signal peptides, carrier peptides and neurotransmitter inhibiting peptides. Overall cosmeceutical peptides trigger wound healing mechanism that activates fibroblasts in response to fragmented chains of elastin and collagen. Peptides increase collagen production to improve skin appearance, resulting in smoother skin.

(VI) Growth Factors

Epidermal Growth Factor (EGF) stimulates epidermal growth and is used in the treatment of burns and excision wounds, where it accelerates re-epithelization. Transforming Growth Factor (TGF) stimulates normal skin growth and cellular growth and repair. TGF exerts positive regulator effects on the accumulation of the body's extracellular matrix proteins. TGF is also a mediator of fibrosis (repair tissue formation) and angiogenesis (development of new blood cells) and it promotes the healing of wounds.

(VII) Others

(a) **Vitamin C**

- Necessary for hydroxylation of procollagen, proline and lysine.
- Deficiency results in purpura, keratotic follicles and bleeding gum.
- It is a water soluble antioxidant.
- Used effectively to stimulate collagen repair thus diminish effect of photoaging on skin.

(b) **Vitamin E** (alpha tocopherol)

- Major lipophilic antioxidant in plasma membrane.
- Decrease erythema, edema, sunburn cells.
- Formulated as potential nano cosmeceuticals.

(c) **Panthenol:** Found in skin cream, lipsticks, lotions and hair preparation.

(d) **Lipoic acid:** It is free redical protector and antioxidant.

(e) **Dimethylamino ethanol:** Used as dietary supplement and associated with improving mental function and enhancing physical performance.

(f) **Glutathione:** Decrease glutathione amount.

(g) **Peroxidase:** Shows anti-bacterial activity.

(h) **Polyphenols:** Act as anti-inflammatory.

CHAPTER 11...

GENERAL COSMETIC EVALUATION

Skin Sensitization and Sensitivity Testing:

The substances that induce inflammation are class irritants. There are two types of irritants:

(a) Primary irritants; cause inflammation on first contact, contact may be for several hours.

(b) Secondary irritants, there are harmless on first contact but cause inflammation on repeated contact and inflammation becomes more severe with progressive contact.

[Contact urticaria means local oedema (swelling) and erythema (increase blood flow) at the site of application. Contact urticaria may be allergic or non-allergic].

Sensitivity Testing:

For detection of potential primary irritation Draize test or its slight modification is used. Experiment animals like Albino rabbits are used.

Test substance may be applied to:

- Intact skin
- Abraded skin
- Lightly scarified skin.

A patch can be applied for 24 hours and sites are examined at intervals and changes are assessed and recorded.

The skin of rabbit is more susceptible than man. But these testing lead false positive and false negative results. If there is no reaction in any of the animals, the same test should be performed on 10 human volunteers, applying test substance on the skin of the forearm.

As per Indian standards, test can be carried out on Guinea pigs or rabbits. The cosmetic to be tested is pasted on 2 cm^2 area of animal skin. Area are shaved to remove hairs and to get better results. The vehicle or base to be used in cosmetics should also be painted on the animal skin as control.

If there is no reduction in any of the animals, test should be carried out in 10 human volunteers. If there is no reaction in human volunteers, cosmetics can be considered free of irritant potential.

On humans, sensitivity testing of cosmetics can be performed as diagnostic or as a prophetic test.

(i) **Diagnostic Test** is intended to discover whether the cosmetic used has caused dermatitis.

(ii) **Prophetic Test** is done to assess whether a new cosmetic should be placed on the market or not.

(I) Patch Test

Place about 0.1 to 0.3 g of cosmetics under test on a piece at cotton and apply to skin of arms, thighs or back. Cover the patch with cellophane and seated with adhesive tape. Apply several patches at a time. Some patches may be of similar cosmetics of other brand and known to cause no harm to the skin. There similar cosmetics acts as controls. These patches are allowed to remain on the skin for 24-72 hours.

If there are no reactions, the same patch may be reapplied to the same place or a fresh patch may be applied.

This is continued till,

(i) Either a reaction is produced under one or more patches OR

(ii) Investigator is confirmed, that no reaction will occur.

Sites of patches should be examined after 30 minutes of removal of patch.

Patch test reactions usually are graded as,

No reaction	–
Erythema only	+
Erythema with papules	++
Papilovasicular	+++
Ulceration/Necrosis	++++

(a) Open patch Test

In case of cosmetics containing higher amount of potential irritant like hair dyes, shampoo, hair tonics patches should be not sealed.

These tests are performed on sensitive skin like bend of elbow, skin behind ears. The site is inspected after 24 hours.

If there is no reaction, test is repeated once more on same site, if still no reaction is there, test is repeated third time.

If no reaction is observed on third application, the person is not hypersensitive.

(b) Prophetic patch Test

Investigator should perform test on him and once get satisfied, he can select ten subjects. Investigator should take concerns of volunteers. For full scale prophetic patch test, 200 normal subjects are used. Test cosmetics are applied for one to five days.

The patch sites are examined and observations are made. Subjects are observed for 3 more days for development at any late reactions. After 7-10 days, patches are again applied to the same area of those subjects who did not show reaction to the test. A well established cosmetic in market is used as a control.

If there are no reactions or one or two reactions out of 200, new product can be placed on trial scale on small community of 10,000 persons. Initial test should be done on 50 volunteers, if any volunteer shows the reaction; the number of volunteers can be increased to 200. Prophetic patch test may be covered or open. It is suggested that incidence of more than one in 10,000 may not result in safe cosmetics.

The report of patch test should be include:

(1) Concentration of chemical/agent.

(2) Alcohol used.

(3) Site of application.

(4) Number of days, the patch was left on the skin.

(5) Period after the removal of patch when observations are made.

(II) Repeated Insult Test

To overcome some of the shortcut of prophetic patch test, repeated insult technique can be used (It is a modified prophetic patch Test). This test involves application of finished product or chemical in concentration same as in finished product.

Test involves application of 0.5 g/ml of test sample to the skin of batch or upper arm. Maintain test material *in-situ* for 24 hours. Allowing 15 to 20 minutes after the removal of the patches, readings are made and the reactions recorded. The test subject is allowed 24 hours of rest and second test patch can be applied to a different test site.

Following 10 individual exposures, the subject is given rest of 10 to 14 days. After this, retest application can be done and a comparison of reaction following retest with the average reading of 10 original applications, permits conclusion of test substance for its sensitizing propensities.

(III) Photopatch Test

Certain substance is not harmful but become harmful when exposed to sunlight. Substances that absorb light wavelengths between 300-800 nm have potential of phototoxicity. So this test should be performed.

(1) In this test apply test substance in duplicate. After 24 hours, one of the patches in the pair, exposed to sunlight for 30 minutes.

(2) One more site without any application of test substance should be exposed to sunlight or UV (i.e. normal skin site). This site acts as a control.

(3) After further 24 hours, patches are opened and examined.

(4) If the patch not exposed to light and the skin area exposed to light do not show reaction but the patch site which has been exposed to light shows reaction, the test indicates that substance is phototoxic.

(5) If no reactions are observed on patch sites and control site the substance may be taken as non-phototoxic.

(IV) Test for Sensitizing Potential

An individual is not likely to be allergic to a substance but may develop hypersensitivity on repeated exposure. So the test involves application of patch reputedly in the same 200 volunteers after an interval of 10-14 days. The number of persons who will show positive reaction will represent the sensitizing potential of the substance study.

(V) Use Test

In use test, the cosmetic to be tested is actually used and its adverse effects, if any, are observed. In this test, 15 volunteers should be asked to use the cosmetic and they should make 15 application of it. If there is no adverse reaction, cosmetics can be released for trial.

(VI) Restricted Consumer Test

After the cosmetic has passed the test for irritant potential and sensitivity potential, it may be released in the market in a limited scale. In case of any adverse report, cosmetics should be further tested.

INDEX